A Harvest Passion

EMILY MURDOCH

Copyright © 2016 Emily Murdoch

All rights reserved.

ISBN: 1535321709
ISBN-13: 978-1535321709

DEDICATION

To my grandmother, Elizabeth Thomas. A woman who knows no equal, and yet has found friends wherever she goes. A woman who loves her acre of paradise, and yet travelled around the world to explore other beautiful gardens. A woman who never claimed superiority or seniority, and yet who reigns as the much beloved matriarch of our family.

Granny, thank you for all that you are and have been to us.

And to Joshua, my husband, my rock, my strength, my support.

CONTENTS

Acknowledgments	i
Chapter One	1
Chapter Two	10
Chapter Three	19
Chapter Four	28
Chapter Five	37
Chapter Six	49
Chapter Seven	58
Chapter Eight	68
Chapter Nine	77
Historical Note	85
Other Books	86
About the Author	87

ACKNOWLEDGMENTS

Thank you Endeavour Press for supporting me to this, the final book of this series. To Joshua, who has never tired of my efforts. To my parents who not only edit but encourage. And to my readers who have followed me faithfully.

CHAPTER ONE

A loud thump by his ear awoke Leo Tyndale with a start.

"I thought you would want to join us in attending church, would not you, sir?"

It took a few moments for Leo to remember exactly where he was. At first, he had thought that he was still aboard the ship, as the gentle sway had rocked him to sleep – but then he blinked once more, and realised that rather than sitting in his own quarters on the ship, he was instead lying in a rather uncomfortable bed in a guesthouse in a little English town called Sandercombe.

Another loud thump hit the thin wooden door that separated Leo from the rest of the world. "Sir?"

"Yes – yes, I am awake, thank you," said Leo as he pulled his legs out of bed, and winced slightly as he stretched them. Six months of living on a ship will do that to you, especially when, Leo thought to himself, you are over six feet tall. But as he stood up slowly, he realised that unlike his quarters on The Zephyr, he could actually stand up straight here, and the floor underneath him was not going to shift at any given moment.

"We'll see you downstairs in ten minutes, sir," said the voice through the door. "'Tis not far to the church, but we would not want you to get lost in Sandercombe your second day here."

Receding footsteps were the only indication that Leo was now alone, but he welcomed it. Being entrapped on a ship with any sort of people, regardless of whether they were pleasing and lively individuals, was enough to drive someone like Leo, who detested the sea, completely insane. And yet, he had arrived – though if he was to determine his whereabouts with the weather, he would have supposed that he was still in India. Hot streaming light poured into his room through the window, and he could already feel beads of perspiration gathering across his temples.

But there was no time to stand and ponder life's greatest questions; to be absent from church was not something society would approve of, and Leo did not want to stand out in his new home town. Not on the first full day that he was in it, certainly.

There was a looking glass above a ewer with a pitcher of warm water beside it, and Leo gladly availed himself of it and his shaving kit that had travelled all the way to India with him five years ago, and been a trusty companion all the time that he was there. Of course, he was more accustomed to shaving in a nearby stream than in this more civil manner, and Leo almost jumped to see his own face looking back at him. Five years of living in India had trained his eyes never to expect to see such pale skin – although to any Englishman, Leo's skin would have been described as dark and tanned, thanks to those Indian heatwaves he had endured.

It did not take him long to shave off the unkempt beard that he had neglected on his journey back to his homeland, and five more minutes were all that were required to dress himself in the trappings of an English gentleman. The cravat was the only thing that gave Leo trouble: not a decoration that was particularly useful in the humid climates were he had been. After knotting his own thumb into it the first few times, Leo eventually managed to create something that looked halfway respectable, and there was no time to consider a seventh attempt. He could already hear the church bells calling in its flock.

"Good morning," Leo said in his deep voice as he came to the bottom of the stairs in the guesthouse. Several people stood around, evidently waiting for him, but he did not flinch or colour. He had seen more than enough to cause any man to flinch in the slums of India, and the disapprobation of a few gentlemen and ladies was not enough to ruffle him.

The guesthouse owner, Mr Chives, did not agree. "Well," he said smartly, his hands clapping together before his portly waistcoat, "now that we are all here, we shall go."

Leo followed the gaggle of people out, and exhaled deeply as he strode into the sunlight. Surely England's summers were not so hot, he thought, for this was almost unbearable! Thankfully the walk to church was but minutes, and even the Reverend was not standing outside in the blazing sun to greet his parishioners.

Inside, Leo could not but smile. It was so good to be in an English church once more; a church that had more history in its walls than most of the cathedrals of Europe. Though this church was but a small one, it had all the beauty and elegance that Leo looked for when he came to commune with his God.

A man pushed past him, and Leo took a step backwards out of his way and almost stood on the long skirts of a young lady's dress.

Quick apologies were murmured. "My sincerest apologies, my good lady, I did not intend any harm."

The lady scowled at him, and strode away, blue satin skirts swishing across the stone slabs of the aisle. Leo swallowed. There was much that he clearly had to learn about society's polite addresses, something that he had never particularly been good at anyway. As he looked around him, he could see that there was a clear hierarchical system for seating in the church, and his gut clenched as he realised that to sit in the wrong place was to immediately mark himself out as a fool – and worse, an outsider.

Gentry were clearly at the front, Leo thought as he glanced from the front of the church to the back, and the poor at the back; but there seemed to be some sort of system for tradespeople of left to right . . . and where did that leave him?

"Good people, it is such a blessing to see you this fine morning."

Leo swallowed. The Reverend had spoken, and voices in the congregation were quietening down. He had to seat himself, and he had to do it now. The pew to his left had only one occupant, and a quick glance at her attire pointed her out as a relatively wealthy woman. He sat without thinking, and breathed a sigh of relief.

"Good morning," Leo whispered to his companion on the pew, before she turned around to stare at him. It was only at this point that he realised that it was the young woman upon whose skirts he had only just stepped.

Her hazel eyes stared at him for a moment, and then she turned back to face the front. Leo breathed out a silent sigh. So much for making a good impression with the townspeople of Sandercombe this morning.

The heat may have overpowered others, but for Leo Tyndale, this was nothing compared to the scorching summer that he had just endured. Nonetheless, he was still struggling to keep his eyes open as the vicar droned on.

". . . such a rich and fascinating story." The Reverend paused for breath, and Leo shuffled in his wooden pew uncomfortably, hopeful that this marked the end of the sermon. But it was not to be. "This reminds me of a tale I once heard . . ."

Leo slumped once more, fighting the temptation to pull at his cravat that had been finished off so tightly – as was the latest fashion in London, he had been told – that it was painful. He tried to loosen it slightly without catching the eyes of any of the parishioners. After all, he had only arrived in Sandercombe the evening before.

Hot, thick light seemed to stream through the stained glass windows, and Leo clenched his jaws together. It was fortuitous that he was seated behind a young gentlewoman in the largest bonnet he had ever seen; if he was lucky, none of the townspeople would have seen Mr Tyndale, lately returned missionary from India, yawning.

The sermon was never going to end, he thought dismally, and he closed his eyes – just for a moment – and remembered longingly where he had been at this time yesterday. Why, at eleven o'clock on Saturday the 13th August 1814, just twenty-four hours ago, he had been standing at the brow of a ship as it came into Southampton Port.

Shouts had rung out in rough voices, and Leo had ducked as a brown faced sailor marched past him with a heavy anchor in his grip, three other man helping him with sweat dripping down from his face. The spray of the sea crashed against the side of the boat of which they had all been residents for the last six months, and Leo instinctively put his hand to the side to steady himself as the waves rocked them.

"Almost there, Mr Tyndale, sir," called Captain Browne, beaming as he strode across the ship's deck in the August evening glow. "Should not be long before we are properly docked, and you can enjoy the feeling of solid ground beneath your feet again!"

Leo smiled, and bowed, but said nothing. His attention was still caught by the vista that was before him: England, at last. It was hard to believe that it was five years since he had beheld its shores.

It was just as hard for anyone who would have been looking at Leo Tyndale at this moment to believe that he was a man who hailed from these very shores. Tall, with dark hair and dark skin tanned beyond anything an Englishman would accept in polite society, there was a fierceness in his gaze that never left his eyes, no matter who he was speaking to. His eyes were a dark green that flashed when provoked, which was rarely, as all those who had travelled with him from India could testify.

Some whispered that he was a rich merchant, and others that he was a soldier on the run from his time stationed out in the colony. If anyone had asked him, Leo Tyndale would have told the truth: that he had been a missionary in India these last five years, and only the death of his parents and an invitation which he could not refuse would have brought him back.

As Leo gazed out to the shore, Southampton was still as busy as he remembered it – perhaps even more so. The hot sun was beating down on gentleman and tradesman alike, even though it was almost eight o'clock in the evening, by Leo's reckoning. He looked up at it, eyes squinting, with a broad smile across his bronzed face; still the same sun as the one that had beaten down on him in India. It was good to know that some things never changed.

Shouts and cheers rang out on ship and shore alike as Leo heard the splash of the anchor, and the many other travellers with whom he had journeyed moved forward, impatient, desperation in many of their eyes as they tried to be the first to step onto the Regent's British soil as soon as possible.

Leo started – his reveries of the day before had almost dragged him down to sleep, and it would certainly not do for the new school teacher to slumber during the sermon. He looked round, pushing the hair out of his eyes, desperately trying to see if anyone had noticed.

All eyes, he was amazed to see, drifted to a half closed position, as the Reverend at the front continued speaking, a man who could quite easily have been bottled as a cure for insomnia, Leo thought with a slow smile. All, except one woman. The woman seated beside him.

Her hair was brown, and pulled tightly under her bonnet. Leo could not see her eyes, but her face seemed to be following the Reverend's every word; indeed, now Leo looked more closely, he could see that her lips were moving, repeating the words that the vicar extolled. No one seemed to be with her. She was quite alone, and the heat did not seem to be bothering her in the slightest.

Of course, Leo reminded himself, he had been gone five years from England. Although such a thing as a woman being completely ignored by her fellow parishioners would have been scandalously rude when he had last been here, England had changed a great deal now that the Regent sat on the throne.

He had received the strongest reminder of this, Leo recalled, just last night as he looked for a stagecoach to take him from Southampton to his new home in Sandercombe. As he had sat in The Dolphin, the only inn that he could find of any repute, a pewter bowl full of steaming stew of uncertain origin had been placed before him. He had ignored his reservations about the slightly suspect meat, chewing down on it instead of asking questions that he probably did not want to know the answer to, and almost groaned with delight when a large tankard of ale was brought to his table.

English food. English ale. English voices around him, chattering in their groups about whether the reports of Prince George's last party were true, and if the French were really going to challenge Russia once more, and if that bakery round the corner still did those delicious tarts. Leo had never missed England when he had been apart from it, but now? How could he ever have left its blessed shores?

Leo started as countless bodies moved; the Reverend had finished his seemingly unceasing monologue and all were now standing to sing the final hymn before they were released from the cool of the church and into the baking heat of the August heat. None better than he could describe this as a true Indian summer.

As their voices were raised in song, a few eyebrows were also raised at the newcomer's deep bass voice that soared below theirs sweetly following the melody. Leo was none the wiser. He glanced to his left, but the young woman was still facing straight ahead, as though he did not exist.

And then the service was over. Leo relaxed as the hustle and bustle of leaving the church started to brim over into quick conversations and gentle chatter. There was nothing that the English loved to do more than gossip with their neighbours.

And yet, he noticed, no one had approached himself, or the woman by whom he was seated. He turned, and smiled at her.

"Good morning," Leo said, trying to remember the niceties and pleasantries that were absolutely no use in India, but were the only valued currency in English polite society. "May I introduce myself?"

The young woman glared at him, her hazel eyes flashing slightly as they moved into a golden beam of light.

Leo smiled weakly, and ploughed on. "My name is Leonard Tyndale, and I am the new school teacher here in Sandercombe."

It was evident that she had heard his words, but there seemed little recognition of them. She sat stiffly, clearly uncomfortable, and yet did not move away from him. It was almost as though she were a cat watching a mouse, waiting to see when he was going to make his first mistake.

Leo swallowed, and tried again. "Do you have any children at the school, Mrs . . ?"

That got a reaction. "You are not so clever nor as smart as you think yourself, Mr Tyndale," snapped the woman, eyes flashing now with anger rather than sunlight. "You may be new to this town and you may think that the quickest way to ingratiate yourself with the local population is to take their stance and deride me at every opportunity, but let me tell you that there is nothing that you can say, do, or think of me that has not been said, done, or thought of me before."

"My dear lady," stammered Leo, unaccustomed to such fire from someone he had only just met – let alone a woman – but he was not able to stem the flow of her words.

"Indeed, your very originality itself speaks more about you than anything that could escape from your lips." She took in a great breath, and shook her head with a furrowed brow. "It is regrettable that you should disappoint so quickly upon a first meeting, but there it is. Good day sir."

She rose, stood on his foot as she moved past him along the pew, and strode out of the church. Leo sat as though struck by one of the monsoon rains that had overwhelmed him the first time he had seen them. Despite her animosity, and perhaps for that very reason, Leo smiled. What a surprise; what a change had been afoot in England for a woman to speak so to a man. It was refreshing, and yet Leo was slightly hurt by it. For some reason, and Leo could not put his finger on exactly why, he was drawn to her. She stood, as he did, in a sea of people and yet totally alone.

CHAPTER TWO

Leo Tyndale threw back the door, and coughed as the stifling heat and dust of the school room flew towards him.

"By God, how long has this place been left empty?" he muttered to himself. Throughout his long sea voyage, he had been planning the first ever lesson that he would give the young boys in Sandercombe, a lesson that would inspire them to new heights, that would open up vistas of understanding previously hidden from them, that would make them love learning as much as he did.

He had arisen that Monday morning an hour early so that he could arrange the school room as he liked, his lesson burning in his memory – but to find the school room almost abandoned and the door nailed shut instead of merely locked was the last thing he had expected. Of course, the fact that he had been unable to remove the face of a certain young woman from his memory had nothing to do with the hours that he had spent awake in the dead of night, and no bearing whatsoever on the tired lines and bags around his eyes.

Leo stuffed his hand in the pocket of his waistcoat, and pulled out the letter that had dragged him from one side of the world to the other. In it, the strong hand wrote of a thriving and energetic town called Sandercombe, full of friendly families and young boys that were desirous of learning; it spoke of a school full of the latest textbooks and modern approaches to learning; it painted a picture of a rather idyllic situation, and the temptation to return back to his country had proved too great, as Leo had sat in the boiling heat of India.

And yet here he was: standing in a school room that had clearly been untouched for the last three months at least, in temperatures just as hot, with but an hour until the boys arrived to meet their new teacher.

Leo sighed. There was nothing for it. Pulling off his tailcoat which he had had furiously scrubbed and cleaned for what he had hoped to be his fine debut, he threw it down onto the dusty desk, and picked up the broom that was leaning against the blackboard.

As he moved up and down the rows of chairs trying to move as much of the dust and soil as he could from the room, Leo tried not to let his wandering mind meander to the woman who he had sat next to in church the day before, but it was impossible. Was this the sort of woman that England was populated with now? Was he to be harassed and harangued at every street corner?

Leo chuckled to himself. It didn't matter that he had been living abroad for the last five years, and he couldn't name a single politician that currently sat in Westminster: he only had to meet her for five minutes to know that there was no one else quite like her in all of England. She was quite unique, and those hazel eyes seemed to surface in the pool of his mind whenever he wasn't careful.

"Who are you?"

There was a boy standing in the door frame staring at Leo with an unashamedly curious look, seemingly stuffed into breeches and a coat that were far too small for him. Leo straightened up over his broom, and smiled.

"Good morning, young man," he said, bowing. The

child did not move. Leo began again: "My name is Mr Leonard Tyndale."

A slightly frightened look came over the boy's face and Leo had to control his own to ensure that the smile that he felt was not apparent to the boy. He clearly recognised the name of his new school master.

"Mr Tyndale!" A hurried and untidy bow followed this as the boy reached up to take his cap from his head, his voice echoing in the large empty room. "But sir, you're . . . you're cleaning the floor!"

Evidently this was not deemed compatible with the status of teacher. Leo sighed, and leaned the broom against the nearest desk. Was he to teach sense as well as science?

"I am indeed cleaning the floor," he said brightly, "because for us to clean out our minds of all ignorance and fill them with knowledge and wisdom, we must likewise seat ourselves within cleanliness."

The boy could only have been about eight years old, Leo would have guessed, and did not seem to understand that an adult could speak in such a way to a child. But then again, Leo reminded himself, he was not the sort of gentleman that most young boys of Sandercombe would see. Tall, with dark hair and even darker skin, with hands that were clearly roughened and calloused by hard work, and yet dressed in the elegant and sophisticated clothes of a man of education. Leo knew that he bridged many worlds – English and Indian, learner and labourer, a man of the world and yet a man who didn't really belong anywhere. If he could see himself with the boy's eyes, he probably looked almost frightening; definitely not a man that belonged in the sleepy English town of Sandercombe.

"Do you want . . . I would like to offer any assistance, Mr Tyndale, if you require me," the boy said, standing up slightly stiffer, and offering up a small smile.

The smile was returned. "Thank you," replied Leo as he picked up the broom once more, "I would be most grateful, Master . . ."

"Clement Anderson," said the boy in a rush, his small smile having grown to a beam. "I'll go and fetch some water, Mr Tyndale, sir, and I can wash the desks."

Leo did not have time to reply; before his mouth was even half open, young Clement Anderson had scampered out of the doorway and off into the blazing sun. But two minutes later he had returned, as good as his word, with a large pail full of well water, and a scrap of rag that Leo suspected had once been part of the lining of his jacket.

Clement did not need any instruction, and he happily chattered away about how excited he was for lessons to begin once more. Leo marked him down mentally as a boy who preferred learning to the hard work outside the school room.

"Though of course, I don't really know who else will be coming in today," continued Clement as he wrung out the cloth over the pail. "It could just be me, after all."

Leo was in the middle of imagining that he had been able to grab the young woman with the hazel eyes as she had tried to stride away from him in church, and had been able to understand exactly how he had inadvertently offended her, and was brought back to the baking hot school room with a jolt.

"I'm sorry," Leo said apologetically, "I was quite somewhere else, and this heat is certainly not helping matters."

It only took him three or four paces to reach the windows, and he rolled the sleeves of his white linen shirt up as he struggled to open up the frames. They had been closed for quite some time, but there was no water in them to swell them up in their panes. The muscles in his arms throbbed, but the windows were forced open – though if he had been hoping for a sweet refreshing breeze to come through, he was sorely disappointed.

"Now," said Leo, turning back to Clement, "what was it that you just said? I do apologise for missing it the first time."

Clement clearly did not mind. "I just said that it could be myself, and myself only that comes to lessons today, though I do hope a few others come in."

Leo blinked. The thought of no one turning up to his school room had not even occurred to him. "I do not comprehend you," he said slowly as he picked up the broom once more. "Why would you be the only boy to come into school today? I counted at least twenty boys yesterday in church, and most of them looked around school age."

Now it was Clement's turn to stare at his teacher in confusion. "Mr Tyndale, sir, it is harvest. Most of us will be with our families, bringing it in before the autumn rains come – I was only allowed to come to school today because my mother says I need to get me an education."

Leo sighed. Of course. Sandercombe was surrounded by the lush golden fields that promised to give a splendid harvest – if they could bring it in quickly enough. How could he have forgotten in the five years that he had been away that for many people, education was just a secondary consideration when it came to feeding the family, and losing the harvest this late in the year would surely leave some families at the mercy of starvation, come winter.

Your very originality itself speaks more about you than anything that could escape from your lips.

Leo almost physically started. His mind was clearly not in the school room, but back with the young lady in the church. Why could he not rid his mind of her? Why did she continuously push through into his thoughts?

In the time it took for him to shake his head and sternly tell himself, completely silently, that he was here to teach, not to become distracted by the beautiful eyes of an angry young lady whose husband would undoubtedly not take kindly whatsoever to his imaginings, three more young boys had arrived into the school room, and were clearly so well trained by their parents that they immediately started to help Anderson with cleaning and clearing up the room.

Two hours later, the five of them were nowhere near finishing, and all of them had taken off jackets, hats, waistcoats, and rolled up sleeves. Leo wiped his brow with a dusty hand, and sighed. So much for his inspiring first lesson.

Casting his eyes around the room, he saw that Anderson, his younger brother Gilbert, a small boy of about five that announced himself only as Robert, and a sulky boy almost nearing adulthood who had not given his name at all, were all seated on some of the desks at the front, swapping bits of food between them. Leo sighed. It must be lunch time.

"So."

The four boys looked round at him as he spoke that single word, and Leo smiled. He had missed teaching.

"So that I can learn a little bit more about you, and a little bit more about Sandercombe, why don't you tell me about the different people in the town?" Leo sat beside the oldest boy, and smiled, receiving returning smiles from the two Anderson brothers and Robert. The unnamed boy remained stern. Leo tried to calm his breathing – due, no doubt, to the hearty work that they had all been engaged in. Nothing to do with the hope, stirring slightly, of discovering more about one young lady of the town in particular.

"Well, there's Reverend Parker of course," started off Clement Anderson, who was swiftly interrupted by his younger brother.

"And his wife Reverend Mrs Parker!"

Leo smiled. "I think that's just Mrs Parker, Gilbert."

Robert piped up in a high voice. "And there's Mr Hennicker, he's the local magistrate and he has three dogs!"

The two Andersons and Robert prattled along quite happily while the older boy munched on his sandwich, and Leo mindlessly interjected every now and again to make a comment, or encourage them to keep going. No matter how many people they named, however, none of them seemed to fit the description of the young woman with hazel eyes – who was not the reason that he had begun this exercise, Leo tried to convince himself. He was curious, that was all, about the new town where he had come to live. None could begrudge him curiosity.

"And that's it, really," finished Robert with wide eyes as he threw out his chest to impress his new teacher, half eaten apple forgotten in his hand.

"Tis not!" Clement beamed proudly. "You've forgotten Miss Royce!"

Robert coloured slightly, and Leo readied himself for an argument. "Miss Royce doesn't count," responded Robert in a whining tone. "The strange lady left Sandercombe!"

"But she came back." These words were spoken by the older boy, and Leo raised his eyebrows to hear how deep his voice was. Nearer adulthood than he had thought.

Clement frowned slightly. "Well, I suppose so." He seemed to be considering something. "But my Papa said that it would have been better for her had she stayed away, after what happened."

"She's rich enough to do what she likes," intoned the older boy, his gaze never shifting from his quickly disappearing sandwich.

"I don't care how rich she is, she's strange," said Robert in a matter of fact tone that only children can really get away with.

Leo smiled at him fondly. "What makes her strange, this Miss Royce?"

Robert frowned slightly as he thought, and then offered, "She is a nice lady. Her parents were very rich, and they lived in the big house where she now lives."

"Miss Royce – Hestia Royce, her name is – was orphaned a year ago," said Clement in a very important voice to Leo. "And she went away to get married to another rich person – "

"Mr Quinn," the older boy interjected. A few flies had swarmed in through the open windows, now that the scent of food had been unleashed, but the boys didn't seem to mind them. Leo remembered the scenes of flies that he had seen in some of the streets of India, and ignored them too. He had sat through worse.

Clement scowled petulantly, his adult tone completely disappearing. "Horace, I was talking!"

Leo filed away the name, and wiped his brow with his handkerchief. Please God, let this be the hottest part of the day, he thought.

Horace shrugged and opened his arms as if to tell Clement that he could continue, but Robert spoke first.

"She always looks at me in a most peculiar way with her hazel eyes, as if she knows what I'm thinking."

Leo's eyes widened slightly. It appeared that he had managed to track her down from right inside his own school room: Miss Hestia Royce. It was a beautiful name, one that fitted her eyes and demeanour perfectly. Of course the boys of the town would consider her strange – this was England, after all, and society expected demure and polite young ladies, not women who snapped at a man sooner than she had met him.

Leo swallowed. If he was going to find out more about her, he should ensure that the boys never guessed why. "So where do Mr and Mrs Quinn live now?"

Robert shook his head. "There is no Mrs Quinn."

Confused, Leo replied, "But Horace said – "

"She went away to get married, but she came back without him," said Horace dully. Bored of the conversation, he clambered down from the desk, and strode out of the school room into the haze of the heat.

Leo could almost taste the confusion on his tongue. "And so Miss Royce did not get married after all?"

"No, Mr Tyndale," chorused the Anderson brothers along with Robert.

Leo swallowed. "That will be all boys – I greatly appreciate your hard work in bringing the school room back under control, but I am sure your parents would not mind having you for the afternoon to help with the harvest. Off you go, and I will see you and as many of your friends as you can bring tomorrow at nine o'clock sharp."

The three boys scampered off, and Leo even caught sight of Robert pulling his linen shirt off over his head in relief as they were covered with the boiling heat of the sun.

But Leo was not thinking of the four young lads that he would be teaching the following morning: he was cringing inwardly at the terrible faux pas that he had forced this Miss Royce to endure the day before. It had not even occurred to him to look for a wedding ring on her finger – he had just assumed that she was married, and so would have children at the school. He had meant no malice in his words, but of course she must have thought he was aware of her sorry history, and was mocking her.

And a sorry history it was too, thought Leo as he pulled on his tailcoat reluctantly, adding another layer upon his skin so that he sweltered even more. To leave your home town to be married only to be returned, unwed? What in God's name had she done.

CHAPTER THREE

When the clock chimed thrice, announcing to all the world that it was indeed three o'clock in the afternoon, Hestia yawned. Her eyes had barely left the minute hand on the large grandfather clock that had been placed in the corner of the drawing room since before she could remember; round and round she had watched it, until it had once more reached its apex, and proudly told the world of its achievement.

The ticking of the clock was the only sound that she could hear, and it was the only thing that moved. The heat made frantic activity unbearable as it was, and Hestia sighed with boredom. Another day, another hour, another minute alone and waiting for the next minute, the next hour, the next day.

She was lying on the chaise longue, dressed in the lightest cream cotton dress that she could find, hair pinned atop her head to keep it out of her eyes, and she sighed.

Closing her eyes, Hestia thought about the summer before this one. Admittedly, the temperatures had been nothing near so overpowering, but she had had friends in the town and they had spent almost every day together. That was the summer that the three girls had had their marriages arranged, and Hestia sighed bitterly as she lay to think of the excitement that she had felt at the time. Mr Isaac Quinn was by far the most eligible bachelor that she had ever known, and it was she that he wanted.

In her mind's eye she could still see the gleam of the sun on his brilliant white hair as he turned to smile at her.

"Miss Royce," said Mr Quinn in that deep and calming tone that he always had. "I have waited a long time to be able to meet you."

Hestia had curtseyed, almost unable to take her eyes from the man before her. She had heard of the Duke of Daventry's youngest son, heard of his charm and his elegant manner, but the man that stood before her was unlike anyone she had ever met before.

"The pleasure is all mine," she had said, with a smile that she seemed to have no control over. "Welcome to Sandercombe."

"I am just sorry that it has taken me so long to visit," replied Mr Quinn smoothly, "now that I see that such beauty dwells within it."

And she had blushed, that such a handsome man could speak to her thus. Yes, her parents had been rich, and arguably influential in Sandercombe – but what was Sandercombe to London, to a Dukedom, to the Royal Court?

The courtship had whirled by, faster than Hestia could understand, and they were engaged! The invitations to their wedding had been written and engraved, and as they were sent out to the postman Hestia had held one in her hand, gazing at it as though it were not quite real:

You are cordially invited to the wedding of
Miss Hestia Royce

to

Isaac Quinn
at Badanholt Church of St Mary
on June 18th at 2pm

Badanholt, the seat of the Duke, was to be the place where Miss Hestia Royce would become Mrs Hestia Quinn. Hestia could recall exactly the feelings of trepidation and fear and excitement and ignorance that had flown through her mind that evening of the seventeenth of June.

And it had all been for nothing.

The clock chimed the quarter hour, quieter and less forceful, but just as triumphant. It would have made any other person jump, but Hestia had spent every day for the last five weeks sitting in her drawing room, waiting for the day to end. She could probably time herself to the hour with near perfection.

Five weeks. Had it really been that long? It was hard to keep track of the days, despite her regimental following of the time that passed. In many ways, that day when everything changed could have been yesterday, for all that she was able to forget about it.

The day had been bright, and the church had been full, and the welcoming face of a Reverend had been barely visible at the very end of the long aisle. Hestia had paused for a moment in the doorway of the church, looking in. Her parents had died months before from fever, and so she knew that she would be walking down the aisle alone – and yet she had not realised what a strange and lonely path it seemed to be.

Music; the congregation rose to greet her, eyes turning to stare at her, more eyes than she had ever seen in one moment all pressing down on her, waiting for her to move. Hestia frantically searched them, looking for those dark brown eyes that always seemed so out of place with Isaac's white blond hair. For a moment, it was as though he was not there.

And then she caught them, serious, and flickering between her and an unseen point. Hestia remembered the relief that she had felt, shoulders relaxing, because though she was to walk up the aisle alone, she would walk down it with her partner for life.

Yet each step had felt like knives, and Hestia's discomfort only rose the closer that she was to the altar. Something was wrong.

She was not able to put her finger upon it until they were facing each other, her wedding band encircled by his fingers as the Reverend led him in his vows.

"Repeat after me," the Reverend had said. "I, Isaac Quinn, take you, Hestia Royce, to be my wife."

It was at that moment, that hesitation, that instant when he could not meet her eye, that she knew.

The dropping of the golden ring and the running out of the church with no backwards glance to the woman that he had abandoned there was mere detail.

Hestia cringed as she sat up, desperate to try to distract herself from the path that her thoughts were taking, but it was impossible. Five weeks ago she had stood at the altar before the man that she had believed had loved her, and watched him run from her with his hand clasped around another woman. The day that she had returned to Sandercombe, without husband, without reputation, and without explanation was one that was seared into her memory forever.

Striding around the room, Hestia ignored the heat as best she could as she tried to calm her frantic thoughts. She knew what everyone in Sandercombe must think, she knew exactly what was supposed of her: she swallowed, even when she thought about it. *They thought that she was not a maid.* What other reason could a young man of impeccable breeding and family have given for leaving the rich and arguably beautiful Miss Hestia Royce at the altar?

Hestia threw herself back onto the chaise lounge, and affixed her eyes determinedly on the grandfather clock. If that was what they wanted to believe, she thought furiously. It was at least less embarrassing than the truth.

KNOCK KNOCK KNOCK

Hestia started, and then relaxed slightly as she realised

that the explosive sound that had interrupted her thoughts was just the knocker on the front door of her house. And then she blinked. Who on earth would be calling to see her?

She rose, and wandered lazily to the window. It was too hot to move any faster, and besides, she knew that it would be impossible to see who it was from there – and yet she did so, more out of familial habit than anything else. It had been the joke that she and her father had shared: as a child, every knock at the door would be followed with the instruction for her to go to the window to see who it was. The joke had never tired, even now she was alone.

KNOCK KNOCK KNOCK

The explosive knock repeated, and Hestia furrowed her eyebrows. No one came here, not to see Miss Royce, the scandal of Sandercombe. It was a miracle that they still permitted her to attend church, let alone walk the streets. Who could be so desperate to see her?

In the middle of the drawing room, Hestia stood, indecisive. Surely it was a mistake. They must have the wrong house. Strengthened by the knowledge that she would not have to speak to whoever it was for very long in order to illuminate them of this fact, Hestia swallowed and strode forward.

The hallway was narrow yet light, thanks to the beautiful furnishings that her mother had chosen. The door lay but two steps before her. Hestia stopped.

Eyes closed, she tried to push down the heat that was threatening to overwhelm her once again, and reached out a hand to where she knew the handle was. It opened, along with her eyes.

"Good afternoon, Miss Royce – and before you speak, you must allow me to apologise."

Hestia almost gasped to see the insolent man who had been so rude to her the day before at church standing tall and proud before her, a hand outstretched as though to physically stop her from speaking if she tried to.

"Young man, I do not know who you are," she began stiffly, "but – "

"Then let me introduce myself." The man interrupted her, and smiled, his white teeth dazzling compared to his dark and tanned skin. Even the hand that was stretched towards her was rough and brown. Who was this man?

But Hestia stiffened. Her curiosity could be satiated elsewhere. "I do not have time for nonsense, sir, and so I suggest you return to your home."

Her clipped words were uttered quickly, and she turned to push the door to once more, but a strong grip clutched her arm suddenly and she breathed out in shock.

"I am sorry." The man was tall, taller than anyone she had ever seen before, and his hand was gripped tight on her wrist, preventing her from moving. "In India there is no such thing as British reserve, and I have somewhat taken on their habits, more so than I had perhaps realised."

Hestia stared from the strong brown fingers emerging from the linen shirt that encircled her slender wrist to the dark eyes in the face of the man who seemed to show no sign of letting go.

"Do you intend to drag me off to India in order to teach me this wild social sphere, or am I to be permitted the use of my arm again?" Hestia spoke tartly, but her ire seemed not to affect him in the slightest.

The man smiled. "I am blunt, Miss Royce, and I so will quickly reach my reason for visiting. I wish to apologise for my ill-chosen words of yesterday. I have since learned that you are, in fact, unmarried, and I was foolish to speak without thought."

Hestia coloured, her cheeks rushing with red that she hoped she could blame on the heat of the day. "Rudeness is not the same as ignorance, but both are deplorable, especially in a teacher," she spat out, twisting her arm so that the gentleman – if he was one – was forced to relinquish his hold on her. "Do not be alarmed, you are not the first and I dare say you will not be the last to dishonour yourself with your brashly chosen words, but for my sake and the sake of women everywhere, I ask that you try to extend a modicum of brain power to your mouth before your lips overrun you."

Rather than being abashed, as Hestia had expected the man to be, she seemed to be having the opposite effect. His eyes flashed green, and the smile that had been disappearing broadened once more.

"Miss Hestia Royce, you are quite unlike anyone I have ever met," he said slowly. "I am Leonard Tyndale, the school master that has recently joined Sandercombe – and I like you."

Hestia blinked. This was not how the conversation was supposed to go: there was not even supposed to be a conversation!

"You have evidently come to the wrong house," she said, her voice slightly dry. "I bid you good day, sir, and I hope that you find what you are looking for."

Once more she made to close the door, but now it was Mr Tyndale's foot, and not his hand, that was preventing its closure.

"I have definitely come to the correct house," he said, his deep voice getting quieter and his smile unwavering. "Miss Royce, I would like to spend some time with you, as the other outsider of Sandercombe."

It was as though there was a gentle hum to the world that Hestia had previously never noticed before. The birdsong that had been present in the trees, the hum of the bumblebees collecting the last nectar before the autumn appeared – all faded in the hum that she did not seem to understand.

"Outsider?" She whispered, staring at the tall man who seemed determined to wander in to her life.

Mr Tyndale nodded. "I will not pretend to know you, or presume anything more of you beyond that which you tell me; but I have enough intelligence, Miss Royce, to know that you and I were seated in that pew in church because no one else would be seated near us. I am a stranger, a man who has lived in foreign lands longer than you could imagine; you are an island here in Sandercombe that no one wants to visit. It would be pleasant, I believe, to be an outsider with another, rather than alone."

The man spoke strangely, like no one else she had ever met. Hestia found herself staring at him without fear, and without embarrassment. His clothes were indeed those of a gentleman, and yet the cravat tied beneath his neck was in an awful state. Dust and dirt clung to his boots as though he had been striding through mud all day, and there was something about his eyes . . . some depth to them that she had not seen in another human being.

For a moment, as she looked into those green eyes, they seemed to turn dark brown just like Isaac Quinn's.

Hestia took a step back as she started. Mr Tyndale looked at her, but made no movement. She glanced nervously at his eyes once again, but they were green now, not dark.

This was madness, she thought wildly. This man could be anyone – he could be a murderer for all you know, and have gained the position of teacher here by lies and treachery.

And yet: he was right. He was the only person to visit her in the last five weeks. Being a pariah in the town where you grew up was a lonely affair.

"I find you highly suspicious," she said finally in a quiet voice, staring up at the tall Mr Tyndale.

He shrugged. "I would be surprised if you felt otherwise."

The moment hung between them, and then Hestia made her decision.

In a quiet movement of cotton, she stepped back. "When I want you to go, you go," was her only warning.

Something highly akin to a knowing smile danced

briefly across the lips of Mr Tyndale, but he nodded gravely and stepped forwards into her home. Hestia's eyes followed him, unable to break away, shutting the door without looking at it.

If she had, she would have noticed a figure move out from behind a tree and hurry towards the centre of Sandercombe with a tongue full of gossip.

CHAPTER FOUR

This was not what Leo had expected.

Every step that took him further into Miss Royce's home felt strange, as though he had forced his way there through false pretences. Try as he might, the fact that he was now completely alone with Miss Hestia Royce, a woman that seemed to beguile and confuse him in equal measure with every moment that he spent in her company, could not help but muddle his mind.

"I presume that you are thirsty?"

Miss Royce had not turned when she had spoken to him as she led him to what he presumed would be some sort of seated area. She pushed open a door, and Leo found himself in what appeared to be a room of dazzling light.

"Mr Tyndale?"

All of the confidence that Leo had when he had knocked on the door to Miss Royce's house seemed to disappear as he stood in the most incredible room that he had ever seen. The walls, the ceiling were made of glass, with pure sunlight dancing through, and the brightness was almost overwhelming – and yet the heat that he had expected was not there. Chairs woven from wicker were spread throughout the room, which now Leo looked more closely was only made of glass on three sides, the fourth wall comprised of the stone that the rest of the house was built from.

"Tea, Mr Tyndale, tea?"

Leo started. Miss Royce was staring at him suspiciously, and he was almost certain that she had asked him a question. "What is this place?"

Miss Royce's hands were folded before her and she spoke in a dry and slightly bored voice. "This is the garden room, something that my father had designed for the house after a trip to Holland. It was created for my mother, who loved the garden, and who could not always enjoy it in inclement weather. Now: would you like some tea?"

Leo bowed his head. "I would be quite happy with some water, Miss Royce."

She stared at him; those hazel eyes that had been burned into his memory scouring his face for something that he knew not. Leo stared back; it was as though he was unable to turn away from her, and she from him.

It was then that he was thankful for the burnished tan that the skies of India had given him over the years, for it hid the colour that was seeping into his cheeks. What in God's name did he think he was doing? This woman was alone in this house, save for him, and if her reputation was not already damaged enough, here they were, unchaperoned, completely alone. Yet there was something about her; something that drew him to her in a way that was almost magnetic. He burned to know more of her.

"Water." Her voice was low, and the word she uttered was not given in the form of a question, and yet Leo found himself smiling awkwardly. He wanted desperately to be seated in one of the chairs. Never before had his height put him at a disadvantage, and yet this woman seemed to tower over him.

Without thinking, Leo sank into the nearest chair and

found its comfort far superior to the one in his lodgings. "Water," he repeated, with an awkward smile.

He had expected Miss Royce to ring for a servant, but with a scowl and shake of her head that made her hair shine in the sunlight, she swept out of the room, leaving him alone.

Surely, Leo thought, there was someone else in the house with them, even if they were just a servant – and yet, he thought suddenly, it had been Miss Royce herself that had answered the door when he had knocked, no servant harkening at his call.

Could she really live here, all alone?

His cravat felt too tight, and Leo tried to loosen it, knowing that the knot was already destroyed. This was madness, he thought to himself: he had travelled the world, lived in strange lands, learned a whole new language in order to speak to peoples who were nothing like him – and yet this woman, from a small town in England, could mystify him and make him feel as awkward as a boy of seventeen.

"Now, Mr Tyndale," Miss Royce swept back into the room with a small teacup and saucer that was, Leo saw as they were handed to him, filled with water, "why don't you explain just why you feel so discomforted?"

Leo's eyes snatched upwards, and caught her hazel eyes that were full of laughter. "Miss Royce," he spoke slowly in his deep voice, "I do not think that I have ever come across anyone quite as observant as you."

"Few have," replied the lady curtly as she seated herself opposite Leo. "And yet most at this point would make their excuses, and depart. You have not."

Leo stared at Miss Royce. She was sitting quite calmly, and yet there seemed to be an edge in the way that she spoke that belied a certain confusion, a tension.

"I will admit, without a desire to offend, Miss Royce, that having lived in India for five years I have faced much fiercer challenges."

Miss Royce smiled, and Leo was astonished to see how much it softened her expression. "Fiercer challenges? Am I to be compared to a tiger, perhaps?"

Leo laughed, and moved the teacup to his lips to take a refreshing sip. "Tigers were far from the greatest challenge that I encountered, Miss Royce, and by far one of the least memorable of all the adventures that I could regale you with."

"India," Miss Royce said slowly, rolling the word about her lips in a way that Leo found intensely distracting. "I barely know it – save its geographical location, of course. Tell me: which adventure would I find the most thrilling?"

Despite the drink of water that he had just taken, Leo found that his mouth was uncommonly dry. It was not the five years that he had spent abroad, he decided silently. Miss Hestia Royce was unlike any other woman that existed, whether it be in England or in India, and he was finding himself mesmerised by her just as the snake charmers mesmerised their captives.

"Thrilling?" His voice was slightly raspy, and he availed himself of the water in the teacup once more. "I do not know you, Miss Royce; how am I to know your tastes in this matter? How can I choose the story that will most delight and astonish you?"

It was the pitter patter that was so traditional between ladies and gentlemen in an English drawing room, but this was no ordinary lady.

"Do not flatter yourself, Mr Tyndale," said Miss Royce slowly. "You may find that none of your stories bear any interest to me whatsoever."

Leo swallowed, but knew that he would not be able to stop himself. "Miss Royce, are you always so . . . so brusque with the people that you entertain in your home?"

The words had only just left his lips and Leo winced at them. Here he was, attempting to make amends for his rudeness not twenty-four hours before, and he seemed doomed to repeat himself.

And yet Miss Royce did not seem alarmed, or offended, or even surprised. "Yes," she said shortly. "But as you are the first person to step through my door in five weeks, I suppose I could be out of practice."

A moment hung between them. It seemed to sparkle in the sunlight, and Leo was not entirely sure what emotion he could feel stirring in himself, let alone in Miss Royce's eyes.

"So." Miss Royce's voice was softer now, and Leo had to shake his head slightly to break the power of that moment over him. "Tell me something of your time in India."

When Leo had first stepped onto the boat that would bring him back to England six months ago, he had felt as though every single moment of the five years he had spent in India would entertain and delight each person that he told it to; such wonder, such an exotic land, such danger that he had experienced.

And now he felt as though anything that he offered to this beguiling woman would not be sufficient to match her own wonder and danger.

Leo searched his memory, discounting encounters with thieves and tigers that would have caused soldiers in His Royal Highness' army to faint: none of those would do.

And then he remembered.

"About four years ago," he began, almost nervously, "after I had only been in India a six month, I decided that I would take a trip into the unknown, with one of the local lads to guide me. I had heard of a temple being buried by trees, overcome by their roots to such an extent that the trees themselves had become the walls, the ceilings, the very essence of this temple."

Leo took a slow and deep breath, and as he caught her eye he saw, to his relief, that she was listening to his every word. "It was a long journey, I was told, and yet I was confident that I could do it, despite the heat, despite the overwhelming desire to stay indoors and do nothing – and so we left, with my guide beside me. It was only after a week's worth of trekking that I realised that India's definition of a 'long journey' was perhaps a little different from my own."

He paused. The sunlight pouring through into the glass room was dazzling his eyes, but Miss Royce seemed completely unaffected.

"It was night," he continued, with a sigh. "The sun was about to rise in not more than five minutes, but I took the chance for peace, and quiet, and the cool. My guide left sleeping, I ventured not ten yards from our tent when I saw, as if emerging from the mist by magic, the temple. A soaring arch demarked the entrance way, and there, under its zenith, a small monkey."

Miss Royce gasped, but ever so slightly, before recollecting herself and readjusting her face into a more unassuming, uninterested look.

Leo smiled: partly at her, partly at the memory. Then his eyes drifted away to focus on the garden as he remembered that moment. "It had in its paws a small glass jar, one much alike those that we have here for jams and preserves. Inside the jar, as I could clearly see, was a large fruit, a delicious succulent one that I have never had the pleasure of seeing in England. One of the monkey's paws was clutched around this fruit, inside the jar, but each and every time that it attempted to remove its hand with the fruit intact, it couldn't. Its fist was too large when holding the fruit, and the monkey would not let go."

Turning his dark eyes to Miss Royce, Leo smiled. "And there he sat, for above an hour, desperately trying to have his fruit, and yet the harder that he tried, the more impossible it became. And when we left him there, with his fruit and his jar, he was still clutching at the fruit that he could see through the glass, and feel with his paw, but never taste."

Silence hung between them, and Leo was almost ashamed to admit that he was desperate to see some emotion on Miss Royce's face. She looked at him blankly, as though she had not even heard him.

"Of course," Leo said hurriedly, "for many people they are not interested in such things, and – "

"I have scarce heard anything so powerful in my entire life." Miss Royce's voice was not gentle, as such, but the ferocity that usually accompanied her every syllable had disappeared, and Leo stared amazed as he watched her lean forward in unbidden interest. "tell me; was much of your time in India like that?"

Leo tilted his head to one side as he considered. "Perhaps without the intensity of that experience, of course, but in that vein – yes, Miss Royce. India is a place of mystery and magic, of which I am still deplorably ignorant. I do not think a lifetime would be sufficient to learn of all its secrets."

"And yet you have returned," countered Miss Royce with a smile that could almost have been described as shy. "Your time in India, then, has come to an end?"

"I would never rule out my return there," replied Leo, almost discovering his own feelings about the place as he spoke. "India has a part of me that I did not even know existed, until I lost it to her. I left it on the shores of Bombay when I boarded The Zephyr, and I think it will be waiting for me there if, or when, I return. I do not think that the harvest of souls is quite complete."

As though she was unaware that she was moving, Miss Royce rose from her seat and stepped towards the chair that was beside the one Leo was sitting in. She dropped into it gracefully, and leaned towards him, captivated by his words.

"Harvest of souls?"

Leo nodded, twisting in his turn to face her, painfully aware that her alabaster skin was only inches away from his own, albeit far more bronzed. It was all he could do to refrain from reaching out and seeing whether it felt as cold as it looked. "It was a phrase that I heard whilst in training to be a missionary, here in England. The Reverend said that there were places in the world, like England, where the harvest was completed and the entire crop had been taken into the church – but there were other places, like India, where the harvest of souls had not even begun. It is a phrase that has remained with me for a long time."

"It is a powerful one," said Miss Royce gently, a smile curling her lips. Her hazel eyes did not avoid his own now, and Leo found himself bewitched by them. "I had always wanted to travel, when I was younger – my father had taken great pains with me, in order to teach me the different countries of the world."

Leo smiled. He was unsure how he had done it, but there was such a connection between them now, and Leo found that he was revelling in her company. No one else compared to this. "I am envious of your beginnings. I was a teacher before I joined the mission to India, but had taught myself a great deal. Will India be the first place that you go?"

Something unsettled the harmony between them. Leo could not tell what it was, and although Miss Royce had not moved, the light and joy in her eyes seemed to dullen.

"I will not be travelling now," she said, her voice darkening slightly as she leaned back in her chair, moving away from him. "Not now that I am unmarried."

"But you may marry again, in time," responded Leo reasonably, "and then you can – "

"I shall not marry." Miss Royce's words were quick, and curt, and harsh. The magic that seemed to be hanging between them had disappeared, but Leo was still left with the longing to reach out and touch her.

He swallowed. "You may find in time that you meet with another gentleman that – "

"I am afraid that I have quite forgot the time and must ask you to leave." Miss Royce's voice was suddenly harsh once more, and cut across his own words like a knife. She had risen from her seat before Leo had time to reach out and touch that enticingly soft palm that seemed to be so close and yet just beyond his reach.

She had walked out of the door and into the hallway before Leo had time to set down his teacup and saucer, but he strode after her.

"Miss Royce, if I have offended you – "

"I must ask you to leave." Miss Royce had by this time reached the front door, open once more, and she stood back with her eyes cast downwards towards the floor.

Leo walked forward, but stopped when he reached her. Despite his great height, he felt as though she was looking down at him. What could he have done wrong now?

"I am sorry," he said quietly. Her hands had dropped to her sides, and Leo knew that if he just took a step forward, if he just moved his arm six inches, if his head was just that much closer to hers –

But Miss Royce put out her own arm and placed it on his chest, pushing him to the left and forcing him to step outside the doorway. He had not even the presence of mind nor the time to even consider resisting.

"Miss Royce – " Leo started to speak with no thought as to how he could continue, but he stopped as he saw the anger and the bitterness in her eyes. Six words was all she wasted on him before she closed the door in his face.

"I must ask you to leave."

CHAPTER FIVE

Leo swallowed, and tried to ignore the burning feeling that he sensed on the back of his neck. The whispers were harder to ignore, naturally, but the very least he could do was pretend that the incessant stares that were causing a hot flush to emanate from the nape of his neck were entirely non-existent.

The murmurs were careful to make sure that their words did not float up to the pew where Leo was sitting in church, but he was still able to catch small snippets, and as he watched the sunlight pour through the stained glass windows as the congregation waited for the Reverend to begin his sermon, he closed his eyes to concentrate, hating himself for wanting to know what they spoke of and yet desperate to know simultaneously.

". . . in her very house, her poor parents would turn in their graves if . . ."

". . . a week he's been here and it hasn't taken him long . . ."

". . . not the sort of missionary I was expecting . . ."

Leo opened his eyes, and sighed deeply. It was not difficult to make a guess about the conversations' subjects, and he found himself shifting in his seat uncomfortably. It was all coming back to him now, he thought wryly, the gossip and fearmongering of a small English town – there really was nothing like it. Even in India, if a person was to speak about another they would do it face to face, with nothing to hide behind and no way to pretend that it had not been them that had spoken.

The heavy church door opened, and utter silence filled the church.

Leo did not need to look round to see who had entered; she had not been visible to him when he had arrived, and there was no one else that could have had that effect on the whisperers.

And yet he did turn round, despite himself, to catch another glimpse of Miss Hestia Royce. Her cheeks had a coral tinge that told Leo she was more than aware of the consternation her entrance had created, but there was no hint of apology in those eyes, or that strong jaw. She strode forward, her Sunday best blue satin gown moving elegantly around her as she paced, and Leo barely had time to swing forwards to face the altar before she deposited herself in a pew two or three rows behind him.

Before Leo could count to five, the whispers and murmurs had returned, reaching a fever pitch that he could not bear –

"Beloved," creaked the Reverend, smiling from his lectern. "We are gathered this warm morning to thank God for His continuing blessing on us, His people. We shall now sing . . ."

Leo did not think it possible that time could continue at such a leisurely and snail-like pace, and yet that church service seemed to prolong itself into the hours. It was almost a surprise to him when he stepped out of the church door that the sun was still up, and it was not evening. The rest of the congregation had settled into groups of three or four, all over the churchyard, pointed stares and even in some cases pointed fingers marking him out as their conversation of choice.

The cravat that Leo had considered loose an hour before, when he had just arrived at church, was now the tightest bond that had ever been created, and he was desperate to remove it; although he had probably caused enough gossip already. The question was, how in God's name did everyone know that he had visited Miss Royce?

As if she had heard his thoughts, Miss Royce strode past him, looking neither to the left nor the right as she forged her passage out of the churchyard and away from the residents of Sandercombe.

"Miss Royce!" Leo called after her, his momentary thought to detain her and explain that he was not the source of the mutterings that were currently circulating through the town, but it was as though she had wiped him from her memory.

She stopped, she turned, and she stared at him with those hazel eyes seeing right through him. For not a single second did she catch his eye, but instead turned her neck slowly, and then resumed her hurried walk.

It was not an auspicious start to the week. Leo found himself dwelling on that moment all evening, even as he sat in his room and tried to find the tiredness within him that would allow him to sleep. Midnight had been struck by the church, and yet still he could not help but go over and over that moment in his mind, creating new opportunities and re-writing his memories as best he could.

"Mr Tyndale," Miss Royce could have said, "I am sorry, I did not see you there."

"It is I who must apologise," he would have said, "for I fear that a simple confusion or misunderstanding has reached the ears of many, and I would not want you to believe that it was a purposeful slander."

"Purposeful slander? Mr Tyndale, I am sure that it is not within your power to do such a thing." Miss Royce could then smile, gently at first, and then more warmly. She would take a step forward, falter, and then take another. "After all, I know too much of your character to believe such a thing."

And then Leo would find himself before her, with only a hand's breadth between them, and her smile made her hazel eyes sparkle like the dawn dew, and she would look up at him with such passion that –

"This is not helpful," Leo reminded himself, shaking his head in an attempt to remove the delicious image of Miss Royce from his head. "That did not happen."

Yet it was many hours more before Leo's mind would allow him to sink into slumber, and too few hours hence that he was forced to awaken.

Stretching, Leo grimaced to feel the ache in his limbs that had no other cause but his own lack of sleep. It did not take him long to dress in that straightjacket of a waistcoat and breeches, cravat once more tied like a noose around his neck, eat hurriedly, and arrive at the school room, and he was somewhat pleased to see that there was a smattering of students already there, waiting for him. They were laughing, and Leo smiled to look at them. The innocence of children was the same no matter which country he was in.

"Good morning, boys," he called out as he walked towards them. It was only then that it dawned on him exactly what they could have been laughing about, and he only thought of it as their smiles disappeared hurriedly, and embarrassment flushed over their faces.

Leo stopped before them, and tried not to let the smile crack from his face. Surely not. Surely boys as young as this would not be exposed to gossip of any sort?

"Everyone inside please," he said, and after they had all trooped inside obediently he followed them, walking past them to the front of the school room. How was he to tackle this? Leo found himself at a slight loss; this was not anything that he had had to deal with when in India. There asking someone something outright was considered good manners. And yet Leo had not been away from England too long to know that here, blunt and direct questions were not the height of good taste.

The distraction tactic then. "If you would all take out your slates, we shall be practising handwriting."

The expectant groans from every student filled the room, and Leo smiled as he shook his head. "Now then boys, your handwriting will be expected to be at a high level by the time you leave this school, and it shall be a constant tool that you will use regularly when you are grown, and so we practise now. Does everyone have their slate?"

It took around five minutes to ensure that everyone had a slate, and then another five to explain to some of the younger children – not that there were many children at all today, Leo thought, but the harvest comes first, as usual – precisely what a handwriting exercise was.

But after the ten minutes of chaos, order resumed. The scratch of chalk moving slowly over a slate was amplified ten times over, and Leo smiled to see the looks of concentration that adorned the face of every one of his pupils.

All, that is, except Horace. Instead of crouching over his work, as many of the other boys were, he was staring at Leo unabashed, with a curious look in his eye. It was almost, Leo thought suddenly, as though he was attempting to untie a complicated knot, or finish a complex puzzle.

"Horace," said Leo calmly, "do you require assistance?"

It was clear that Horace had not expected to be spoken to, and he looked awkwardly down at his slate. "No, sir."

"There's clearly something the matter," Leo said gently. "What is it?"

For a moment, Leo thought that Horace would not say anything, and return dutifully to his slate, but it looked as though he was weighing up his two options. Finally, he chose, and he decided to speak.

"Mr Tyndale," Horace said quietly, "when did you

know you were in love with Miss Royce?"

Leo had never heard silence like this. Every single boy still had their chalk in their hand, but not a movement did they make. Their eyes were transfixed on his own, and Leo found that his own jaw had fallen open.

"In – in love?" Leo spluttered. "Horace, what makes you say that?"

Horace squirmed in his chair, clearly feeling as though he had made the wrong choice. "I heard my parents talking, and they said that you had made love to Miss Royce, that day that you went to her house after lessons."

"My pa said that you moved quickly," added Robert, "but I didn't know that you had run there, Mr Tyndale."

Even the children thought that he had had his way with her, Leo thought gloomily. Was it not possible for a gentleman to call on a lady, and for them to enjoy nothing but conversation? But he knew the answer to that; he should have thought about his actions before he had called on Miss Royce, because unlike India, in England everything had consequences. No wonder church the day before had been so uncomfortable. So now the whole of Sandercombe thinks that – oh, God, it was not worth thinking about.

"Miss Royce and I are friends," Leo found himself saying, "and friends only."

There was a stunned reception to his words.

"I didn't think girls and boys could be friends." Horace spoke without the air of a question, but Leo answered him.

"It is possible, but it is quite rare." Which is why, he thought grimly, all of your parents are talking about it. Fingers reached up and loosed the cravat, and then threw caution to the wind and removed it altogether.

"So," piped up Robert, "you don't love her?"

This was not a question that Leo wanted to answer – not because he was in love with her, obviously. That would be preposterous.

"Mr Tyndale?"

For the second time, Leo's jaw dropped, and at the same time every child turned their head rapidly round to stare at the figure standing in the doorway to the school room.

It was Miss Royce.

"Hest – Miss Royce!" Leo spluttered, with the boys laughing at him and his confusion. "What are you – I was not expecting – school has just begun!"

Panic and confusion melded together to make his words nonsensical, and he cringed inwardly at the words that he had already spoken. What was she doing here, at his school, now, in the morning? Why did his body have such a visceral reaction to seeing her? And most importantly, how was he to speak to her without even more gossip?

And then instinct took over.

"Boys, I am sure that your parents would appreciate some extra pairs of hands today with the harvest." Leo heard his own voice as though it was coming from a long way off. "I'll see you again tomorrow when we'll go over those handwriting exercises."

The boys did not need telling twice; they scampered out of the school room and into the sunshine – though Leo doubted that all of them would make their way to their parents. Bringing in the harvest was at least as difficult, if not more so, than handwriting.

Miss Royce was still standing in the doorway, unable or unwilling to come in any further.

Leo swallowed. Desperately he wished that he had not removed his cravat, but it would be far stranger to attempt to replace it now. "Miss Royce." His voice still sounded dry, but there did not seem to be anything that he could do about it. Just being in her presence made him feel different.

"Mr Tyndale." Her reply was short, and her voice was quiet. The anger and fire that he had last experienced appeared to be doused, by he knew not what. Her light green cotton gown was pinched around the waist to show off her slender frame, and she was breathing deeply, so deeply that Leo couldn't prevent himself from looking at –

All of a sudden, Leo was not entirely sure what to do with his hands. Wherever he put them – down by his sides, crossed over his chest, through his hair – seemed wrong.

Thankfully Miss Royce interrupted his hurried thoughts. "I was wondering whether you would accompany me on a short walk?"

"Yes," replied Leo, grateful for the excuse to move forward and be closer to her. "Just lead the way, Miss Royce."

The sun was further up now, closer to midday, and Leo felt the sweltering heat prickle his neck as they moved into the sunlight.

"You will need to lead the way," he said, almost apologetically. "I do not know Sandercombe well enough yet to conceive of a convenient route."

Miss Royce was only a few inches away to his left, so he almost felt, rather than saw, the smile. "Do not fear, Mr Tyndale, I grew up in these fields. I shall not lead you too far astray."

For the first ten minutes of their walk, there was silence – and yet Leo did not feel as though it was in any way an awkward silence. If anything, it was companionable silence. As Miss Royce walked, her cotton gown rustled the dying grass, and she picked at the golden seed heads at their very tops.

The route that she had chosen, Leo soon saw, would take them around several of the fields where the people of Sandercombe were bringing in the harvest. He watched as strong arms strained to lift heavy sheaves of wheat.

"It looks to be a good harvest," he said quietly.

But Miss Royce clearly had no interest in the harvest. "I wish to apologise, Mr Tyndale."

"Apologise?" Leo glanced over to her, but those hazel eyes that he was beginning to know so well were facing directly forward, without an inch given. "Miss Royce, I will admit that I know of nothing you need to apologise for."

"Then you are far too polite – and perfect for polite English society," retorted Miss Royce, and she did then look at him for a fleeting moment. "You know full well that I was unnecessarily rude when I asked you to leave my home last week, and I fear that my reaction to your . . . questions was not what it should be."

Leo shook his head. "Miss Royce, you have nothing to apologise for – I was a guest in your home, and my impertinence was reason enough for you to ask me to leave."

Reaching the end of the field, they turned the corner so that the sun was now directly in their eyes.

"And anyway," continued Leo, almost thinking aloud as her hand grazed past his as they walked, causing shockwaves to travel down his arm, "you had only just met me, really. There was no reason for you to countenance such rudeness from a complete stranger."

"Complete stranger?" Miss Royce stared at him with a strange look on her face – something almost akin to disbelief. "Mr Tyndale, in the whole of Sandercombe there is only one other person that is in any way like me, and that is yourself. We are outsiders, and I recognised that as soon as I saw you."

Leo pushed aside a bramble, and shrugged. "I am not entirely sure what makes yourself an outsider, Miss Royce; this is your home, where you grew up and continue to live."

"And yet there is so little that I truly like about it."

Looking over sharply, Leo saw that there was no mockery, no hint of a smile, no joke that danced around her cheeks. Miss Royce was, for perhaps the first time, being open with him.

"Indeed," Leo said gently. "But you must have some interests, some passions that take up your day and invigorate your mind?"

He had no idea where they were going, but Miss Royce seemed to know a path and he willingly followed her, with no thought to distance, or safety, or time

She smiled slowly, and Leo was astonished to see a slight blush wash across her cheeks. This was not the Miss Royce that he had last spoken to. What had caused this?

"Come now," Leo repeated, "what are your passions? What do you love?"

Miss Royce did not answer immediately, but allowed her left hand to fall lazily into the wheat, brushing along the heads that were so industriously being gathered in by the harvesters. After a moment, she said, "I like geography. I would like to travel, one day, and see all of the places that I have learned about."

Leo nodded, and broke into a smile. "That is, I think, a passion that we share. It was not long into adulthood that I was champing at the bit, ready to explore a new country, a new world."

"There is little that fascinates me more," admitted Miss Royce, her hazel eyes lit up with an internal blaze that was increasing with every moment. "It seems unbelievable that there are distant shores, out there, in the world, with different trees lining the paths and diverse creatures clambering along them, unlike anything that I have ever beheld. Different languages with different dress, different politics and different architecture: everywhere one looks, a new discovery to be had, every bite a new adventure."

"It is as though you have stepped into my very mind," Leo breathed happily. They had turned, the path before them twisting as though unsure which direction it would take.

Miss Royce swallowed, the smile lessening slightly as she realised just how unguarded she had been. "But I will not – I do not think I ever will travel. Sandercombe is my home, much as I dislike it, and this is where I'll stay."

"Dislike it? This quaint little English town, you dislike?" Leo shook his head. She was so close to him now that he could smell the rosewater that she had dabbed that morning behind her ears. His fingers longed to reach out, to bridge the gap between them. "That does not make much sense to me."

"It may not make much sense to you, but it does to me. The gossip here is not so much a disease, but an epidemic." Her response was curt, and Leo tried to catch her eye to see whether he had offended her again.

"Gossip?" Leo stared at her, understanding starting to dawn on his features. "Miss Royce, are you telling me that you . . . that you are aware of the talk about . . . about you and myself?"

Miss Royce laughed, and shook her head with a bitter look on her face. "Mr Tyndale, are you really so dense? Of course I am!"

"Then why come?" Leo asked, bewildered. "Why come to the school room to see me? Why take me here," and he outstretched his arms to indicate the wide open fields, the harvesters not half a mile from them and in plain view, "to be watched and gossiped about once more?"

She laughed now, and shook her head slightly. "Mr Tyndale, what use would my life be, what pleasure would I gain from believing the very rumours about myself which I know to be false? Why should I ignore all instincts and avoid a person with whom I wish to converse, just because another rumour will begin? I cannot live my life by the rules of other people, by their expectations and their opinions! The gossip shall start no matter what I do!"

Leo stared at her in amazement. "You speak as though your future is already set."

"It is," Miss Royce said ruefully. "The only way that the world knows how to talk about women is by describing them in relation to the men around them! Walter's daughter, Isaac's jilted bride, Leo's mistress – do you think that I'm ever given a second thought, once they have put me in a box and labelled me?"

"You are so much more than that!"

"You don't have to tell me," snapped Miss Royce, but with a smile on her face as they turned another corner. "I am not just some woman who was left at the altar, and I will not be defined by the men around me. I am my own person, and it is time that the people of Sandercombe treated me as such."

Miss Royce sighed. They had reached a fork in the path, and she stopped.

"Mr Tyndale," she said, turning to face him so that the golden sun almost gave her a halo. "I . . . I find it difficult to be open with people now. Not just yourself, but anyone really, even those whom I have known almost a decade. Not after what has happened."

Leo's heartbeat quickened. "After what has happened?"

"The point is that I find any questions difficult, and I reserve the right not to answer them." Miss Royce's answer was curt, but as she moved to turn away, she gasped. Leo had taken one of her hands in his own.

"Miss Royce," Leo said quietly, not releasing the delicate fingers that squirmed in his own, "what happened? What happened with that man that you were engaged to? What was it that changed you so much?"

Her eyes were wide and she stared at him in apprehension. "Nothing that I want to share with you."

Her twisting fingers soon found their release as Leo was unable to keep a grip on them without injuring her, and she strode off, her gown flying behind her.

"You need to tell someone!" Leo called after her, ignoring the looks that his shout was creating from those harvesting in the fields. "Mark my words, Miss Royce – you have to allow yourself to be open with someone eventually!"

She did not turn around, and soon disappeared from his sight.

"Someone like me, for example," Leo said wistfully.

CHAPTER SIX

"Good evening, Mr Tyndale," hailed a woman that Leo did not recognise, "and thank you for taking such pains with my son!"

Leo bowed, but the woman was swept away by her partner as the beat of the dance quickened, and he was given no chance to enquire as to which child in his school belonged to her. Not that she would probably have heard him, he thought to himself. The Sandercombe Assembly rooms were not built for the large community that had grown up around it, and the stifling heat of the day was added to by the stifling heat of fifty or perhaps even sixty dancers weaving in and out, cheering at every quarter the musicians that sweated profusely as they played.

As he walked around the large oak panelled room, smatterings of conversations drifted into his ears.

"And I heard that they shall have to be married immediately – "

"Well they'll have to marry now!"

The heat was overwhelming, and Leo cursed at the formal attire that he had once again been forced to wear. Was there no end to this English snobbery when it came to dress? Was he ever again going to be comfortable in his own clothes?

"The damned French will have no other options before long, mark my words."

Leo nodded at the group of gentlemen tutting and shaking their heads, but received little response, as though their eyes glazed over him completely.

He had almost decided not to come, the long school days punctuated by bursts of Miss Hestia Royce disturbing his mind, and he had returned to the guesthouse exhausted; but five years in India had not quite quashed his English sensibilities, and to miss the very first event of the new season was something that even he could not bring himself to do.

And so he was here. Despite the crush of people there was only one pair of eyes he sought. Was she here? Had she come?

Leo squirmed. The heat of the room was rising, and so was his discomfort. The starched collar was pressing into his throat painfully, and it seemed ridiculous that he was forced to wear four layers – four layers! – in this harvest heat. But if she came . . .

It was another two dances before he caught sight of her, a quiet figure that slipped into a corner directly as she entered the room. Leo smiled. Miss Royce could try and be as unassuming as she liked, but she was never going to fade into the background: not with eyes like green sapphires that flashed like stars.

Leo found his legs were in motion almost before the thought even entered his head, and it was mere moments before he was standing before the woman that he was probably falling in love with, and saying, "Miss Royce, will you honour me with this dance?"

Her flashing eyes did not disappoint, and she glared up at him suspiciously. "A dance?" Her hands unconsciously smoothed down the cream silk of her gown, one that was elegantly made with little embroidered silk patterns layered around the bodice, temptingly attracting Leo's attention.

Her hair was pinned into an elaborate bun just above the nape of her neck, but unlike the rest of the female population of the room, she had not adorned her locks with jewels, or feathers, or ribbons, or lace. Simply attired, Miss Royce shone like the sun in a sky of clouds. None could match her.

"This dance, preferably," replied Leo calmly, but the smile on his face was unsure of his reception. As he watched her eyes glance around the room, he added quietly, "You will gain more attention by standing here at the edge of the room without a partner than packed in the throng of people standing up."

For a moment, Leo paused, waiting for a response. Why was he doing this? Why was he forcing his company, which seemed to be so abhorrent, on a woman such as this? Why are you risking pain and rejection once again? But even if Leo could not admit it to himself, deep down there was a small voice that told him he only had to get her talking for five minutes – five minutes, and he would be able to discover the real passions of Miss Hestia Royce.

Who sighed. "I suppose you are quite correct," she said begrudgingly, holding out an arm.

Leo tried not to let surprise light his eyes as he led the most beautiful woman in Sandercombe onto the dancefloor, although others in the room were not so able. Whispers blew around the room like a dandelion's head blowing in the autumn breeze. Leo tightened his hold on her hand, and a glance told him that her cheeks were now pink.

"What shall we have now?" Leo called out to the musicians with a broader smile on his face than would ever appear there naturally. "A longways country dance would be wonderful!"

"And it shall be given to you!" A musician replied good naturedly, and after a few whispers with his company, they struck up a tune.

As Leo had hoped, as soon as the music began there

was no time to pay attention to the new school teacher and the outcast of the town — there were partners to find, promises to keep, and positions to take!

Leo and his partner took a place in the middle of the set, and Leo smiled. Miss Royce did not say a word and her expression did not change until the top couple began their movement down the set.

"Thank you." Her voice was stilted, but Leo could see by her eyes that the words were honestly meant.

Leo smiled, his nonchalance only half true. This moment seemed to be pulled tight like a violin's bow: one wrong move, one wrong word, and the fragile bird that was Miss Hestia Royce would suddenly fly up into the air again, never to be caught once more. "I . . . I wish to apologise, Miss Royce, for the way that I spoke to you last week, in the hay fields."

Miss Royce arched an eyebrow. "Apologise? You do remember that you are a gentleman, and I am a lady? I was rather under the impression that the fault of any problem always lies in the lady's quarter — after all, we are fickle creatures, and not to be trusted."

"Perhaps that is true," countered Leo, trying to keep serious. This was an apology that he knew he needed to make, throttling cravat or no. "And yet I think in our acquaintance so far, the responsibility for apologies has been predominantly on my side, which I cannot bear."

A smile was the only response that he got, and as they stepped in and out of the line with the top couple and took their step to his right, he opened the subject again.

"Nonetheless: I do apologise. I should not have pushed you to speak of your past that day — or any day. Your secrets are not mine to take, Miss Royce, and your story is yours and yours only to tell, if you should ever wish it."

Leo looked deep into Miss Royce's eyes, and the brittle smile that she had pasted onto her face so easily now faltered slightly. "Your apology, unrequired as it is, is much appreciated. You . . ." And now her voice faltered also.

"You were quite correct in encouraging me to speak of . . . of what happened. I cannot help but disagree that the corner of a field during harvest is the right time to have that particular conversation, but that is must be had, I cannot disagree."

The arc of her arm as it rose and fell, the turn of her waist as she moved around her female neighbour in the dance, the flash of a smile that had far more genuineness and far more spark than Leo had seen before – he was mesmerised, almost missing his cue to circle his neighbour in his turn.

What was this power that she held over him? There was a mystery about Miss Royce, and the closer that he got to her the further it seemed to pull away, tempting him further and further into the depths of her character. She was intoxicating.

"And now that you have learned so much about me," her clear voice broke their silence, and Leo shook his head to bring him down to earth, "it is high time that I learned more about you. What is it that you miss the most about India, Mr Tyndale?"

Leo smiled. "Whenever I close my eyes, even for a moment, images of my five years there rush past them. There is a heady mixture of clashing sounds, roaring waters, a medley of colours so bright that it were as though God himself had used the country as his palette. Nothing tastes like Indian food, nothing smells like an Indian market. Since coming back to England, I will confess that much here seems bland in comparison." He paused, questioning the sense of his continuing, but took a deep breath and threw caution to the wind. "Except you."

The colour that had only just recently vacated Miss Royce's cheeks surfaced quickly once more, but she stepped around her neighbour with her arms aloft and let them fall gracefully as she returned to her place in the set. "But what do you miss the most?"

Leo stared at her in some amazement. "You know, you

are the first person to ask me that since I docked here?"

She laughed, and Leo revelled in that laugh. "That does not overly surprise me, Mr Tyndale. You have to remember that you are in England now, where another person's business is automatically everyone else's – but only if you can discover it through covert means. It would not be seemly to simply ask!"

The dance moved on, and a small glance told Leo that they were almost at the top of the set. It was only mere seconds away, the moment that he could take Hestia – because if he was honest, that was how he wished to address her – into his arms without any fear that she would disappear, or run away.

"You still have not answered," she reminded him, a curious look on her face. "What is it about India that makes you love it so much?"

He did not have to think; it was as though the answer was dancing on the edge of his tongue. "The harvest over there, for the poor, and the lost, and the hungry, and the forgotten. There is so much good that one can do there, so much of a change that can be made to people's lives."

"And that is what you want?" Miss Royce asked quietly, holding out her hands willingly as they reached the top of the set. "To make a difference?"

Leo stretched out his hands, and clasped hers in his own. They felt so delicate and yet so strong, with a fierceness in them that fought his grip just as much as it welcomed it. He drew her towards him, and his breath became short as he grew warm. There was such intelligence in her eyes, such honesty, and such fear, all mingled in eyes that sparkled from green, to brown, to both.

"To make a difference to another person's life is the greatest thing that a person can do." Leo spoke quietly, and Hestia was so close that only she could hear him. "It would be a truly incredible thing, to look back on one's life and to know that it was irrevocably entwined with another."

For a moment Leo knew that he was in very real danger of leaning down and kissing Miss Royce full on the mouth, despite the crowds, despite the room staring at them, despite the beat of the dancing calling them down the line. As he looked into her eyes, he saw that she knew it too, and his stomach stirred. It would just take the smallest movement, and –

Lashes long and dark fluttered, and her eyes were cast down. The moment was gone, and it was as though he had come up from a deep dive. Music seemed to swirl about him like waves, and he realised that they had lingered too long at the top of the set.

"Come," was all he said, and they flew, rather than danced, down the set. Every time their hands separated Leo felt a loss, and every time they joined once more it was a though his very feet had taken wings.

At last they reached the bottom of the set, and Leo found himself out of breath – and not due to any exhaustion.

"It is strange," he said seriously but with a smile, "that you should ask about India."

"I do not think that it is so very strange, considering that the majority of your adult life has been spent there," retorted Hestia, breathing hurriedly but a beam of a smile on her face.

Leo laughed, and shook his head. "Perhaps not – but it is particularly pertinent at the moment. I am thinking about when I should return there, and that time always seems closer the more that I dwell on it."

The smile that had so brightened Miss Royce's face disappeared quicker than the English sunshine. "Return – return back to India?"

"There will always be a new harvest there, of souls and bodies that need a person to stand alongside them," Leo nodded."

"But, but," spluttered Miss Royce. "But you are doing

so much good here! You would so readily leave the school that you only began teaching in a month ago? I can't believe – "

Her words were cut short as she intertwined with her partner and spun, and by the time that Hestia and her partner came to rest once more, Leo recognised the bitter face that stood before him, and his heart sank.

"I did not mean to upset you," he said awkwardly, "and to be honest, I am a little surprised that you feel this so. I – I had no idea that – "

"I have not the faintest idea what you are talking about." Her words were curt once more, but there was far more pain in them than Leo had ever discerned, and her cheeks were flushed, but not with embarrassment. "What does it affect me, you abandoning the town that you have only just arrived in?"

In a swirl of satin she turned as if to leave the set, but Leo broke rank from his side of the dance and stepped into the abyss to stop her, one hand on her arm.

"How many times am I going to have to do this?" His voice was gentle and low, but he could see that Hestia's eyes were not looking at him, but the dozens of eyes staring at them from both sides of the dance. "How many times do I have to watch you stride away in anger and in pain when it was not my intention – and five minutes' grace would give me the chance to mend things once more? Do not let this be the way we part; not again."

Hestia wrenched her arm away, tugging at Leo's shoulder but surely causing more bruising to herself. "It is not – do not think that I am upset on your behalf!" She shot back. Free again, she strode to the edge of the dancefloor towards the table offering punch bowls.

Ignoring the pointed stares and whispers that had once again surfaced, Leo followed her. He felt at this moment as though he would follow her anywhere.

"Miss Hestia Royce."

She sighed, and then she turned to face him, a goblet of

punch in her hand. "I do not wish to speak to you."

"Well that is a shame," was the curt reply she received, "because as you have so recently pointed out to me, we are in England here, where social convention and expectations demand that you stand here and listen to me – and even if it didn't, you should!"

Hestia stared at him as though she had never seen him before, and Leo relented. "You know, it is completely impossible to be angry at you, infuriating woman that you are – and you are, Miss Royce, and I will not hide that from you."

Her eyes had widened even more, but she said not a word and she did not move away, which Leo saw as the only sign that he was to receive that he could continue.

He swallowed. "If you really do not want me to go back to India, then it is much easier to say that, and to say that you would be sorry to see me go than storm off in a petulant rage. It is far too easy to run away from a problem than stand and face it."

Hestia's bottom lip fell open, and she stared at him, tears gathering in her eyes. "Then do not go."

Before Leo could even think of responding her punch had been placed on the table behind her and she had flown from the room, leaving confusion and bewilderment in her wake once more.

CHAPTER SEVEN

Hestia had been sitting on the floor of the hallway for over an hour, and yet still she did not move. The sunlight that was pouring in through the open front door was harsh and close to the midday heat, and yet she did not move. There was a letter in her lap, and tears on her cheeks.

Elegant swirls of penmanship danced across the front of the letter, and she did not need to open it to know that it had been written by Isaac Quinn, the man who had left her at the altar not three months before.

"You have to open it, you know," Hestia tried to tell herself quietly. "You cannot just sit here waiting for it to disappear of its own accord."

She paused, as if waiting to see whether or not she would heed her own advice, but nothing happened. The light blue cotton gown that she had considered to be the perfect choice for another day of heat was darkened where her tears had fallen.

"Hestia," her voice quiet, "there is absolutely no way that you can remain here, seated on the floor, holding in your hands a letter from the man with whom you were engaged to be married. That is just nonsense."

And yet it was so much easier to just sit here looking at

the exterior of the letter rather than look inside it. Who knows what it could contain? What words of solace or of pain had been inked into each line?

Another ten minutes passed, and Hestia shook her head, dashing away a tear from her cheek.

"You are stronger than this," she said bitterly. "Time to read this letter."

The seal on the back was as familiar to her as her own family's, and although she tried to open up the paper without breaking it, the placement on the crease meant that she had no choice but to destroy it to read the words that had been written to her by the man she had thought would be her husband.

Dear Miss Royce,

I cannot tell you how grateful I am for your conduct after the 18th of June this year. Few ladies would have held themselves in such high dignity, and been worthy of the praise that I bestow on you.

Leaving you on our wedding day, with you standing at the altar ready to take my vows of love, is something that I shall never quite forgive myself for – but I rest certain in the knowledge that I would have ruined far more lives than I would have made happy should I have ignored my better judgement, and followed through on my promise to marry you. My methods were inexcusable, but my reasons have every excuse. I did not love you.

You would have been well within your rights to sue me for breach of promise, but I knew from the moment that I met you that you would never have stooped to something like that – yet my gratitude still bears the relief that you did not. Thank you for not holding anger and bitterness against me.

My wife and I send all our best wishes. You must come and visit us sometime when you have occasion to venture from your beloved Sandercombe. I know how much you love it there, and I would not drag you away from it unwillingly.

Yours, still with the affection and high esteem and regard that I hold you in,

Isaac Quinn, Esq.

The tears that Hestia had been so desperate to control overwhelmed her now, and the sobs that she had attempted to hold so close to her chest now surfaced. Salt washed her cheeks, and she abandoned herself to her sorrow for some minutes.

But it was not for the reason that she had supposed it would be as soon a she saw the curl of the lettering of the H on the letter that only one person had ever constructed in such a way. Oh no; not for Isaac Quinn did she now weep, although the hurts of that moment were still raw.

Hestia cried not for the love of Isaac that she had lost, but for the love that she knew was burgeoning upwards in her heart for Leo – a man that was already planning to leave not just Sandercombe, but England entirely.

"Why," she whispered sadly, "does every man that I feel even the slightest affection for decide that there is another that he would rather devote his life to? Another woman, another country – it is the same when the results are examined. They are gone."

It had been three days, three long days since she had last seen Leo, and with each day she had hoped that he would come to visit her. She was not really entirely sure what she was hoping that he was going to say. What could he say? She had pushed him away far more times than any other man would have accepted, and yet still he had been patient with her, still he had listened to her, still he had stared at her as though she was the most important woman in the world.

The day had slipped into evening by the time that Hestia had come to a decision, and it was not one that she felt wholly comfortable with. At the same time, she knew that it would be the only one that, looking back, she could live with.

It took her but moments to move about her home collecting the few items that she wanted to take with her, placing them into her reticule, and so before she really knew what was happening, swept along by the power of her own decision, Hestia found herself walking through the centre of the town past seven o'clock in the evening, on the way to tell Mr Leo Tyndale exactly how she felt about him.

"This is complete madness!" She muttered under her breath. Most of the people of Sandercombe were inside, eating their final meal of the day and sharing stories of their exploits, and so she had the streets to herself – something that she much preferred. She knew that the whole town had been surmising exactly why Isaac Quinn had left her at the altar, and despite not actually hearing their guesses, it was not difficult to jump to their conclusions.

So enwrapped in her own thoughts was she that she did not notice the shadow of a figure watching her path, and so determined was she to reach the guesthouse where he was staying quickly before being spotted, that she did not realise that she already had been.

Pushing open the door, Hestia was greeted with the sight of a good number of the harvesters drinking their well-deserved ale. Her eyes widened as chairs and stools scraped around to stare at her, and she flushed deeply. How had she not thought this through? Surely she should have realised that there would be plenty of people still taking their drinks this early in the evening – many of them, in fact, looked as though they would be returning to the fields for another few hours of bringing in the harvest.

Hestia swallowed. "I . . . I am here to see Mr Tyndale."

She was not sure who she was speaking to really, but to the room at large. She had never visited a man in lodgings before – never visited a man whatsoever, unless you included Isaac Quinn, and his whole family had always been in attendance at such meetings. What was she doing?

"Mr Tyndale?" The guesthouse master, a Mr Chives called out from behind the bar. "Well now, I suppose he would be in his room, Miss Royce – do you know the way?"

Titters and guffaws swirled around the room, and Hestia flushed.

"I do not, as you well know Mr Chives, as this has been my first visit to your establishment – and is likely to be my last, if your hospitality is anything to go by." The laughs disappeared as the steel that lay deep within Hestia surfaced once more. "Now, I wish to have a serious business discussion with Mr Tyndale about the school room, and I would like to have it in private. Is it too much for you to point me in the right direction, or do I need to open every door in order to discover him?"

She could not exactly tell whether the looks she was now receiving were respect mingled with confusion, or distaste mingled with displeasure. Either way, this was not a place that she wanted to stay long.

"Business, eh, about the school room?"

A man that Hestia did not recognise stood up from his stool, and he gave her a short bow which she returned, slightly confused, after nodding.

The man nodded in return. "My boys are at that school, and I'm right glad I am that you are taking notice of our young folk. It's good for them to know that their education is important, Miss, and I'm pleased to see you here. I'll show you to Mr Tyndale's room."

For a moment the entire room continued to stare at her, but then as if God was saving her from further embarrassment and notice, a young lad helping Mr Chives at the bar dropped a pint tankard with a loud crash onto the floor. The shouts and cheers of the men distracted them from the sight of a young lady enquiring about a gentleman of an evening, and gave them something new to focus on. Hestia breathed a sigh of relief.

"I must thank you," she said awkwardly as the man led her up a flight of stairs, their dark wood seeming to creep in, giving Hestia the feeling that she was slowly suffocating. "It was most gracious of you to . . . well, rescue me."

"Say no more about it," the man said gruffly. Hestia could see a large tear down the back of his shirt that had been mended by tiny, delicate stitches. "Young lady like yourself needs a bit of kindness in the world, if you ask me."

The tears that Hestia had been forcing back ever since the letter had been delivered to her door that morning seemed about to surface, and then the man then stopped, and turned to retrace his steps.

"Sir?" Hestia called after him, but he gave no reply and was soon out of sight.

He had left her by just one door, and so she knocked on it hopeful that it did contain the man for whom she had made such a daring decision.

A tall, dark haired and completely astonished man opened the door.

"Hestia – Miss Royce!" Leo Tyndale stared. "What in God's name – "

"It is very breezy out here," she said abruptly, pushing past him, staring at the room that she had stepped into. It was sparsely furnished, as she supposed she should have expected considering where he had come from, but the few personal furnishings that he had chosen seemed to tell her more about Leo Tyndale's character than anything else. The Bible by the bedside was well thumbed and had several bookmarks in, and the mirror above the water basin was dirty, without any care or thought to how its owner would be able to use it.

Although in all other respects clean, the room could hardly be described as tidy; it was as though it was used only for sleeping, and that was all. A bed, a chair, and a chest. That was all that was really there.

Turning, Hestia saw that Leo was still standing in the doorway, the door itself wide open, and his face still showed the same first signs of shock that registered when he had opened the door.

"You'll let the heat in," she said, and then she could not help but smile. "It is good to see you, Leo – Mr Tyndale."

If she had hoped that he would correct her, and tell her with a grin that she could call him Leo, then she was very much disappointed.

"What are you doing here?" His voice was not cold, exactly, but there was no warmth in it, no desire to prolong a conversation any longer than it needed to be. "It is late."

Suddenly all of the well thought phrases and clever sentences that Hestia had created to tell this man, this man that she had only met but a month before, that he was starting to become more and more precious to her each and every time that she saw him, completely vanished.

"I . . ." she said weakly. "I . . . do you mind if I sit down?"

Leo outstretched his arm, indicating the chair, and she sank into it gratefully.

"I know that I must apologise for coming so late," Hestia began, but she was cut off.

"Why are you here?"

Hestia swallowed, and then looked into the almost black eyes of the man before her. "You may not have noticed this about me, but I have a rather prickly personality when I decide to be . . . well, difficult. When you first arrived here, and you were so forthright with me – I am not accustomed to meeting someone as stubborn as myself, someone who – "

"Miss Royce, what is this really about?" Leo's voice sounded tired, and Hestia winced. Why had she convinced herself that Leo would be pining away for her, for lack of seeing her, for the confusion that she always left him in? "You may not have to awaken early tomorrow morning, but I have a school of young boys to teach algebra to, and I would prefer to do so on a full night's rest."

"Why are you making this so difficult?" Hestia said,

the pain that she had been attempting to hide finally breaking forth. "You know, you must know how difficult this is for me to – cannot you see how unaccustomed I am to – "

"Being open." Leo strode to the bed and sat down, facing her. "Hestia, there are few people that I wish to be so open with as yourself, and yet you are the one who has been holding back. It is you, and not myself, that has shrunk away at every opportunity. You and only you have set the pace for our acquaintance, and to be perfectly frank with you, I think that I have danced to your tune for too long."

Hestia frowned. "You are not the easiest person to talk to either, you know: never before have I been asked such impertinent questions, and I think I have borne them well considering the circumstances!"

"Circumstances that I have no idea about!" Leo said with a shake of his head. "No, Hestia, I am sorry. I . . . I want to know you in a way that I have never felt before. You are the first woman that makes me smile every time that I see her, but none of this seems to touch you – and why, I do not know. No one seems to know!"

Hestia's fingers clutched her reticule, and she could feel the letter within it. Was this the moment to tell him? Surely the truth could not be so bad as the rumours that he had undoubtedly heard – surely it would be better to speak out now?

"And you won't tell me," Leo's words cut into her thoughts, and dampened her mood. "And that is your right, Miss Royce. Our acquaintance is but of a short time, and yet I feel closer to you than I do to most people I have known for years – it is as though our souls have met before. But if you cannot tell me this, then there is too much being held back for me to – for us to . . ."

His words faded away, but he did not need to iterate his meaning.

Hestia rose from her seat, her reticule falling to her

side. "I'm not ready."

She spoke with an honesty that made Leo burn even more for her, and he tried to hide his disappointment as he moved to the door to open it for her, letting the woman that was more to him than any other out of his presence.

"I hope that you can tell me," he said softly as she stood but inches away from him. Her eyes were fixed on his, and he stared deep into them as to plant these words into her very mind. "I hope that you can soon, Hestia, because you should know that I am falling in love with you."

Leo was not entirely sure what reaction he had been hoping for with those igniting words, but it was certainly not the response that he received.

"Love?" Hestia sniffed. "I don't believe in love."

"Don't believe in love?" Leo took a step back, almost unaware that he did so, and stared at the woman before him as though she had just announced that she didn't believe in breathing. "Hestia, love isn't something that you can choose to believe in or no; it is an essential force, a fact of life, a current of nature!"

"Love is a choice," returned Hestia quietly, "and if one can choose to love one day and choose not to love the next, then it is a rather fickle and frail imagination of a person. I see no evidence that a man can love a woman truly, without falling away and losing that love as soon as he forgets to choose love."

A moment of silence filled the space between them. Leo could not take his eyes from Hestia's face, and he finally broke the silence.

"What words can I engage to persuade you of the fact of love?" He said quietly. "What arguments have you not already heard to demonstrate that love is the most unchanging force, when it is true, when it is right?"

"I do not think that you can." Hestia's voice was low, but clear as a bell and full of pain. "I do not think any words will be enough."

And that was when Leo knew exactly what he wanted to do, knew the only thing that could not only persuade her, but show her – but dare he?

He took a step forward, bridging that gap between them that had been of his own making just moments before, and smiled softly. "Perhaps, Hestia," and his hand reached out for hers, claiming it as his own, "I do not need to tell you. Perhaps I need to show you."

Shock, confusion, uncertainty filled her eyes but her gasp parted her lips ever so slightly, and Leo could not help himself. Leaning down, he dropped his lips onto hers and kissed her.

Hestia arched her back unconsciously, deepening the kiss, and Leo could not help but wrap his arms around her, bringing her closer to him so that he could feel her warmth. She was nervous, he could tell, but then nerves and excitement were rushing through his body just as much, and he felt as though he was exploring a new country for the first time, one full of soft mountains and silky rivers, ready for discovery.

Leo broke away, realising that much longer with Hestia Royce in his arms, and he would find himself with much less control than he had ever had.

"Leo . . ." she whispered.

He chuckled under his breath. "We seem to be continuously apologising to each other," he said wryly. "Let's not apologise about this."

CHAPTER EIGHT

The smile that Leo Tyndale awoke with on his lips did not last long.

The day had started off so well; pleasant slumbers had followed the heart quickening kiss that had made Leo feel as though the world had paused for a moment, just so that they were not knocked off balance as they had clung to each other.

Sunshine had poured into his lodging room, and although the heat of the day was already rising it did not seem as oppressive as it usually did.

Hestia Royce was on his mind, and Leo thought that the day was going to be good. But he was wrong.

As soon as he stepped out of bed he saw it: a small piece of paper that had been pushed underneath the door to his room, but with his name scrawled on the outside as if to make sure that no other read it.

Instinct told him that this could not hold anything of worth, and yet the hope in his heart told him to ignore his gut – a decision that he would later regret. Stooping down, Leo picked up the paper and unfolded it to see a very untidy scrawl writing words that he would not even consider speaking, let alone commit to paper. And Hestia's name was included throughout it.

Disgust flowed through him like a poison. Was this really the depths that a person could stoop to when a man and a woman who were not related enjoyed each other's company? Was this really the natural conclusion of what two people would do when they had the chance, forgetting propriety, forgetting society, forgetting that they had only known each other for a matter of weeks!

The crude suggestions of what they had done the night before were seared into his mind like a brand on cattle, and no matter what he did he could not remove them. The very idea that he would – that they would – before they were married? It was obscene. It was indecent.

But it was not too far from what he had wanted to do the night before, Leo admitted to himself when he had calmed down. If he was truly honest with himself – and it was not something that he usually had to force himself to do – then in part, his outrage was not only that an unknown person was suggesting that he had made love to Hestia Royce, but also because he wished that they were partially true!

"This is ridiculous," he said to himself as he sat on his bed, the note in his hand. "I want to go back to India. I want simplicity, and this is not something that will make my life any easier. It will complicate everything – my ability to travel, my chance to see the world, and to serve in India, it's all I've ever wanted! The one thing that I was ever truly passionate about."

Leo closed his eyes, sinking back into those familiar images of India that always made him smile, always gave him peace – but it was not the spark and fire of that wild country that flew across his eyes. The laugh as they danced, the glare when they argued, that uncertainty she always had, that constant concern that she should not trust him, and then that glorious inevitability that came when she took another step of faith towards him.

It was Hestia Royce, and not India, that circled round

his thoughts and washed through his soul. Hestia Royce, and nothing else.

It took but moments for Leo to dress himself, and mere minutes for him to decide that nothing was more important than seeing the woman that he loved.

Yes, he knew now that he loved her. When you would rather be with one person, and that one person, even in the dullest place on the Earth, than be without them in the most exotic far off land, then it was time to bind yourself to that person. It was time for that person to know just how important they are.

Leo almost fell rather than walked down the stairs, but he did not pay any heed to the shouts of his landlord as he cried out in surprise, and he gave just as little attention to the people that cried out to him as he passed them in the street. Not even the school room could gain his notice now that he had a purpose higher than any other – and his pupils watched him from the school windows, mouths open.

He was almost out of breath by the time that he reached her house, but Leo could not help but smile. In but a few short moments he would have in his arms the woman that he loves, and then nothing else would matter.

But it seemed as though something else did matter, for before he could even rap on the door to announce his arrival, the front door opened sharply and a hurricane of a woman approached him.

"How dare you – how could you let this happen!"

Leo took a step backwards in self-preservation, and stared aghast at the woman who stood before him. Hestia Royce stood there with eyes like daggers and an angry flush across her cheeks, hair untied and flowing down her back, a shawl around her shoulders despite the blistering heat – but what stood out the most was the piece of paper that was held aloft in her left hand: a piece of paper covered in a scrawl that looked heart wrenchingly familiar.

"Hestia, don't read it," Leo said hurriedly, "don't – "

"I've already read it!" Hestia spat, hair flying in all directions, and she brandished it at him as though it were a weapon. "I've already read it, damn you, and I can never look at you in the same way again!"

"You don't think that I wrote such – that I could have made insinuations such as these, if yours is as the same as mine!" shot back Leo, desperate to defend himself but not entirely sure what he was being accused of.

Hestia laughed bitterly. "Who knows, maybe you did write it! Perhaps you wrote it as a joke, and slipped it under my door! As if I needed another letter that brought me to tears, a second in two days!"

"A second in – a second?" Leo stared at her as her shawl slipped from one shoulder. "Have you received a letter like this before?"

The flush of anger was joined by a flush of embarrassment on Hestia's cheeks, but she soon regained her composure just as soon as she gathered up her shawl and brought it around herself once more. "Not exactly alike, no, but enough to make me realise that all men seem to be the same – all desperate to ruin my reputation!"

Leo shook his head, his feet shifting in the gravel as he tried to regain his balance. "Hestia, you should ignore it. Your reputation is not ruined, and even if it is, what does it matter?"

It was the silence that told him that he had made a huge mistake. Something like betrayal cried out at him from Hestia's eyes, and yet she said nothing.

"I mean," Leo continued, nervously now as he tried to navigate unknown waters with no charts to guide him, "what is a reputation after all, but just what other people think of you? You are so much more than that, Hestia."

Hestia took a deep breath, but when she spoke her voice was not loud, as Leo had expected, but instead very quiet. "I know that I am, actually, Leo – I did not need you to tell me that. What you do not understand is that my reputation is the only thing that I have to my name! I am a woman, you fool, I cannot even own property really; it is seen as just being in my name until I marry, and then everything that I am and everything that I possess becomes my husband's!"

Leo opened his mouth, but Hestia was not finished. Her hand that held the libellous piece of paper had dropped to her side, and the anger was gone completely; but in its wake was only sadness and bitterness, and it tore at his heart to see her so.

"In this world, Leo," she continued, "a woman's reputation, her good name? That's the only thing that I have that's mine, but once it's lost, isn't not something that I can just get back!"

Leo swallowed. "Another day, another apology? I'm sorry. It's hard for me to understand just how important – "

"Yes, it is," said Hestia sadly. "And that's just it. You said that you cared for me, you said that you – you were falling in love with me."

"I am – I have!" Leo moved forward, desperate to break the distance between them, desperate to bring her to him and kiss away the sadness and frustration in her eyes, but as he moved forward she took a step back across her threshold.

Hestia sighed. "Leave me alone, Mr Tyndale."

"Hestia – "

"Leave me alone." Her repeated words were dull, and so was the sound of the door as it shut in his face.

"Mr Tyndale?"

Leo watched the light drift lazily through the windows, sparks of dust floating in the air and glinting off the sunbeams.

"Mr Tyndale, sir?"

There was not a whisper of a breeze, nothing to disturb

the sunlight as it fell slowly to the floor.

"Mr Tyndale!"

Nothing to stop it or prevent it from its purpose. Light was conquered by nothing, and the heat of the day was certainly overpowering, forcing all to bow to its –

"Mr Tyndale!"

Leo started as a small pair of hands tugged at his shirtsleeve. A small boy that he did not recognise was standing before him, large eyes gazing up at him in awe.

"I'm sorry, Mr Tyndale sir, but you were not responding. Could you hear me?"

A faint smile moved across Leo's face, but it was gone almost as soon as it had arrived. "I must apologise young man; my thoughts had wandered elsewhere. What was it that you were trying to tell me?"

The boy swallowed, unaccustomed as he was at speaking with a man of such high authority in his eyes. "I was just saying sir, that we are all here."

Leo raised his eyes, and was astonished to see that the school room, usually so empty with only a handful of boys waiting to be taught, was this morning absolutely packed. In some cases, there were two or three boys to a desk.

"My goodness," he said, standing and smiling weakly at them all. "Where have you all come from?"

The young boy Robert stood up with a smile, and said, "Please sir! The harvest is over now, and so our parents have said we are now allowed back to school, and we'll be here most of the winter now, sir."

"The harvest?" Leo stared at them sadly. Eyes stared up at him, some hungry for learning, some unimpressed with the performance of the teacher so far, others just desperate to take their jackets off to relieve themselves of the heat. Leo sighed. "The real harvest failed this year."

His captive audience did not seem to understand.

"Failed?" A boy that Leo did not know spoke up, confused. "My Papa said that this has been one of the best harvests that he has seen in years – better than the one when I was born, and that was one of the best ever!"

Leo smiled wanly. "I apologise – I spoke of a different kind of harvest. You know, it is possible to sow many seeds but for none of them to grow, even though it looks as though some of them may push through the soil and burst forth into the heat of the summer. Even when you think that you have tended, and cared for, and done everything that you could to make sure that the harvest is strong – even when you are passionate about the harvest – that does not always mean that you can enjoy it."

What am I doing, he thought to himself. These boys understand even less of this than you do.

"Settle down now, boys," Leo said, rather unnecessarily, and he began to pace around the room as he spoke. "I need you all to pay attention. It is with deep sadness that I inform you that I will not be staying for much longer to be your teacher."

"Not staying!" The two Anderson brothers, sharing a seat near the front of the room, spoke in unison, their faces mirroring each other in horror and confusion.

"Not staying," repeated Leo. "It is time for me to move on, and I never promised that I would be here forever.

"But," swallowed the small boy that had awakened him from his doze that morning, "where are you going?"

Leo shrugged. "Abroad. India, perhaps, although I am not sure whether I shall stay there long."

A child raised their hand, and Leo nodded at them. "But you've been to India before!"

"I have indeed, but it is a very large country – far larger than I think even I can imagine," replied Leo. "There is so much of the world that I want to see, and although I have enjoyed my time with you all – "

"You're not going because of Miss Royce, are you?"

Leo started, and looked around the room. He could not see which boy had spoken, but there were certainly some very sheepish looking older boys sitting at the back.

"I . . ." swallowing, Leo tried again. "My acquaintance

with Miss Royce is not anyone else's business, but it is probably common knowledge now that I would have liked Miss Royce to – well, to be my friend, rather than just an acquaintance."

"I think you like her," said Robert quietly.

Leo nodded. "I do like her. She is a strong and courageous woman with a large amount of intellect and an affectionate heart. I do like her."

Robert shook his head. "No, I don't mean like her – I mean you like her. As your wife."

Sadness dripped down the back of Leo's throat, and it was bitter. "As I was saying boys, sadly my time with you is coming to an end. You will have a new teacher by Christmas."

The stunned silence in the room was, although Leo would never have admitted it to anyone else, rather gratifying. He had not thought it possible to be liked so much after being in a place for so little time – and yet, it had been long enough for him to fall in love with the most impossible woman in the world, so anything was possible.

"And on that note, I close the school for today," said Leo in a hurry. "No more lessons today. Out you go boys."

Some went willingly, glad to be free from the school room in the early hours of the afternoon, whilst others went with less gladness in their hearts. Leo had to spent a few minutes consoling the Anderson brothers, and only managed to improve their mood by promising to speak with their parents about a local tutor who would be able to educate them for the nearby grammar school – if they were good, and their parents agreed.

The room seemed cavernous without the scores of boys in it to make so much noise. Leo stood at the front of the room, with the blackboard behind him, and sighed. The end of another era.

As he stepped out of the school room shutting it with the heavy lock that prevented any vagrants staying in it overnight, the blistering heat poured down on him as though punishing him once more. Was it not enough that he had lost any chance of being with –

Hestia Royce.

Leo didn't think. He didn't even hesitate. It took only four strides for him to cross the street, ignoring the barouche that was coming towards him forcing it to swerve to avoid him, and for the countless time he placed his hand on Hestia's arm.

"What on – Leo Tyndale!" Hestia gasped, turned to see who it was who was manhandling her and dropping her reticule in the process.

"This is not the place," he responded curtly, pulling her along with him back to the school room door.

"What are you doing – Mr Tyndale really, unhand me!" Hestia pulled at his hand, and her voice became more frantic when she realised that he was paying absolutely no heed to her words – and even more so when she saw just how many people were staring at them. "Leo, for goodness sake let go!"

But Leo Tyndale was not going to let go – not now that he had everything that he wanted literally within his grasp. Pulling Hestia through the doorway of the school room after opening it quickly, he thrust her forward, shut the door, and pulled the bolt to. It clicked into place. They were locked in.

Leo's smile was broader than it had been in a long time, but that did not prevent Hestia from reaching out her palm and smacking him smartly across the face.

"And just what exactly," she said angrily, "do you think you are doing?"

CHAPTER NINE

"This is ridiculous," said Leo boldly, far bolder than he actually felt.

Hestia laughed, throwing back her head and exposing her delicate throat. "You're damn right it is! What right do you think you have to literally drag me from the street and to lock me in your school!"

Leo reached out a calming hand, and said, "Just hear me out, Hestia – just listen to me."

"While you keep me in a locked school room?" Hestia laughed, her face awash with disbelief. She was dressed all in white, dirt and dust clinging to the bottom of her skirts. "I don't think so; isn't this false imprisonment? Are you allowed to keep a young lady against her will?"

Free from his grip, she strode away from him and towards the front of the school room, her long skirts swishing around her merely adding to her general atmosphere of irritation.

"This is not the place that I would have chosen," Leo admitted, following her slowly, "but there seemed like no greater moment than now for what I have to say to you."

Hestia raised a quizzical eyebrow and stretched out her arms to gesture at their surroundings. "Really? This is the place where you want to – what is it exactly that you want to say to me?"

Leo could hear his heart beating, feel it pumping fear and exhilaration as well as blood through his veins, but he knew what he had to do – what he wanted to do – what he knew, as soon as he had clapped eyes on Miss Hestia Royce, he would eventually do.

"Miss Royce," he said quietly. "Hestia."

The gentleness and softness of his tone made her stop her frantic movement, and stay still, staring at him.

"What?" She eventually exploded, leaning against his desk at the front of the school room.

"Why won't you just listen to me?" Leo retorted.

Hestia shook her head sadly, but with a smile on her face. "Oh Leo, you just don't comprehend, do you? I've spent my life listening to men, being told what to do, where to go, what to say, who to be – that's the life of the daughter of an English gentleman, and I never expected or wanted anything different."

"You should," was Leo's blunt response, but it only widened her smile.

She nodded. "I know." Walking slowly towards the window, that overlooked one of the fields, laid bare now after the harvest had been taken in, she paused for a moment. "So you won't mind if I bring this little conversation to a rather abrupt end."

Before Leo could even think what she was doing, Hestia had pushed a window open and, lifting her skirts above her knees with both hands, had slipped out of the large gap and into the field.

"It's like snake charming this woman!" Leo muttered under his breath as he tried to move towards the door to unbolt it without taking his eyes off her. "She's impossible!"

It did not take him long to thrust wide the door and march through it, and Leo soon picked up the pace as he ran round the school room to the field where he had last seen her. In the distance was a figure in a white dress, walking slowly across the harvested fields in the golden light of the afternoon.

"Hestia – Hestia Royce!"

Whether she could hear him or not, she did not give any sign or indication that she wanted to converse further with him – but Leo was not finished yet. Not until he had said what he knew he must say.

Running in the heat of an English summer, especially one that has continued into the middle of September, was not a sensation that Leo relished, but with his heart pounding he knew that every step he ran brought him closer to the woman that he loved.

"Hestia – Hestia!"

As she turned to face him, her dazzling eyes sparkled in the sun, flashing hazel.

"Do you not understand the subtle hints that I am giving you?" She said laughing. "Honestly, Leo, to look at you one would think that you were – "

"In love?" panted Leo. He saw a faint flush go across her cheeks, and he continued. "Now then, since you have made it so difficult for me to speak to you, I think that you owe me the courtesy of actually listening, rather than running off."

Hestia seemed to consider for a moment, and then she sighed, and turned to face him. "I suppose I owe you that," she said begrudgingly, "and I would much rather talk out here than in a locked school room."

Leo laughed and sighed. "It wasn't locked, just bolted, as well you know. Now listen to these words, Miss Hestia Royce, because I have been dwelling on these for some time."

It was then that some sort of realisation evidently began to dawn upon her, and her eyes widened as she watched him fall to one knee before her.

"Hestia Royce," said Leo with a knowing smile on his face, "you are the most confusing, breath-taking, irritating and beautiful woman I have ever met. No one makes me smile like you do, and no one makes me laugh like you do, and no one makes me apologise like you do!"

"You're going to be doing a lot more apologising if you don't get up soon," she warned him, but he carried on.

"Hestia, I love you." Leo laughed gently. "It seems strange saying it aloud, especially after everything that you have said to me about love – but my feelings for you transcend those basic emotions that take me through each day. You are so different from everything else I know, and I never want to lose you. Will you do me the incredible honour that I know I am completely undeserving of, and be my wife?"

It had to be said for Leo that although he was not expecting an immediately positive response, he was expecting a response of some kind. There was no breeze, and the sharpness of the harvested wheat was digging into his knee and leg. The silence that he received was certainly not what he had imagined, and so after leaving it for a full minute, he spoke again.

"We'll go to India," he said, still on bended knee before the woman that he loved. "You don't have to stay here – we can see the world together, pursue our passions and the things that we love with the person that we love! This will be an adventure for us both."

"No, it will not." Hestia's voice was curt, and she pushed past Leo almost knocking him to the ground as she started to continue her walk away from him. "And you know it will not. I am sorry, Leo, but I will not marry you."

"Not . . . not marry me?" Rising from the ground as quickly as he could, Leo spun around to stare at her. "But Hestia, don't you love me? Don't you care for me, even a little?"

Hestia stopped in her tracks, and whirled around. "How can you doubt that?" Her voice was quiet, with a hint of pain, but also filled with hope. "Leo, I was the one that came to your room, stupid as that may have been, to try to tell you how I felt about you. Do you think that I would have done that unless I had deep and abiding feelings for you?"

Leo took a tentative step forward, and grew bolder when he saw that she did not back away. "So you do have feelings for me?"

"Feelings?" Hestia took his hands in her own, and he could feel them shaking. "Leo, before you can even begin to understand exactly what it means for someone like me to open themselves up to love . . . you need to know what it was that happened before. Between myself, and . . . and Isaac Quinn."

Leo tried to calm his breathing, tried not to show just how much this meant to him. He loved her, and that much was sure – but if he was really honest with himself, could he love a woman that had already made love to another? Did he want to know what had transpired between them? Would it be better to live, and love, in ignorance?

Leo swallowed, and smiled. "Tell me. I love you."

"I know," Hestia replied, "and after keeping it from you, and the world, for so long, I think it may sound like a trifling story now that you hear it – but I cannot over-emphasise the effect that it has had on me."

Leo nodded, his hands still encased in her own. It was almost as though they were the only things keeping her upright.

Hestia sighed, closed her eyes for a moment, and then looked up at him. "I had never met Isaac Quinn when I became engaged to him. My parents knew that they would not be long for this world, not after they contracted cholera, and despite my relative fortune that they would leave me, it had been . . . difficult for me to attract a suitor. I was a prickly individual even then, and successive seasons soon showed me that it was the gentle, rather pathetic girls that would find husbands quickest.

"Isaac Quinn's father is the Duke of Daventry, but as a fifth son there was no fortune for him, and he wanted a quick marriage as his father was threatening to disinherit him. He approached my father, and the betrothal was announced a day later. I was then informed."

"Wait a moment," said Leo, confused. "You were then informed – they told you after it had been announced?"

Hestia smiled wryly. "I am not a romantic, not in the truest sense Leo, and I had none of the strange sensibilities about love that many of my peers seemed to have. My main concern was that upon meeting me, Isaac Quinn would change his mind.

"My parents died soon after, and the date was set for me to become a bride of Daventry. Each and every time that I met with Isaac Quinn – and they were not numerous – I took care to play the part of a very simple, plain, and gentle girl. I think after a while I just was so in the habit of being that person that I convinced myself that I could be that person for the rest of my life."

Leo stared at her. "You were willing to do that much?"

"Many other women have endured worse," countered Hestia sadly. "I consoled myself with the knowledge that my future husband had always treated me with kindness and courtesy, and that was a good deal more than many women enjoyed from their spouses."

"But he left you!" Leo could not help but burst this out, and cursed himself for doing it as soon as the words were out of his mouth. "I am sorry, Hestia, for stating it so matter of factly, but the truth is that he left you."

"At the altar." Hestia spoke dryly, but Leo saw that there was no bitterness in her voice any more. "Exactly where I thought my whole life would change, I went from a marriage of convenience to a jilted bride. Some thought it was because I was . . . impure. Others thought it was because Isaac Quinn had discovered something terrible about me from my past, and thought that he could go through with the marriage and yet found at the altar, in the sight of God, that he could not."

Her voice faltered, and Leo pulled her unperceptively

towards him.

Hestia swallowed, and continued, "I personally thought that he had waited for me to come down the aisle, and found that he did not like me enough to marry me."

"Hestia," chided Leo quietly as he gently released his hands from hers, and wound them around her waist, holding her tightly. "Have you taken a good look at yourself, at your character, at your conduct? You are more than good enough for him – too good, by the sound of it, and I am glad that he was a fool."

Hestia shook her head wistfully. "I wish that I had had your approach to myself, and yet I was not nearly so kind. You cannot imagine what it is like to be left standing at the front of a church in your wedding dress with no husband beside you and the ring lying on the ground where it has fallen."

"No, I cannot," breathed Leo, but he smiled nonetheless. "And you never have to feel that way again. Marry me, Hestia."

Hazel eyes that seemed to be alight from within stared into his own. "Don't you wish to know why it was that he left me there, abandoning me before our marriage had even begun?"

It didn't take Leo long to come to the honest conclusion in his mind, and not much longer for him to speak it. "No. You are Miss Hestia Royce, and I love you as you. I don't need to know the second rate opinions of a strange gentleman. I want this adventure with you, Hestia. Marry me. Come with me to India."

Hestia did not answer, but lifted herself on her toes and kissed him full on the mouth, her hands wrapped around his neck, giving herself – finally – completely. Leo groaned, it was so wonderful to have her in his arms, and the kiss deepened as he tilted her head gently and allowed her lips to fall open. This was what he wanted, this is all he wanted for the rest of his life.

It seemed like an eternity, but it did come to an end.

"No," said Hestia quietly.

Leo almost fell over in astonishment. "No? No! What do you mean, no?"

"No, I will not marry you and come to India with you." Hestia spoke seriously, but she did not make any move to vacate his loving arms.

"Hestia Royce, you would try the very devil!" Leo exploded. "Why – "

"I don't want to go to India," she interrupted, one hand stroking his cheek as she smiled impishly up at him. "I want a completely new adventure for us, one we can share together, with both of our passions – and our passion for each other. What do you say to the wilds of Africa?"

Leo stared, and then he smiled. "You, woman, are going to be a bigger challenge than the wilds of Africa could ever be!"

Sweeping her off her feet, Leo spun her round as her laughs filled the empty field, and as the sun finally dipped down under the horizon, he brought his lips down onto hers for another passionate kiss.

HISTORICAL NOTE

I always strive for accuracy with my historical books, as a historian myself, and I have done my best to make my research pertinent and accurate. Any mistakes that have slipped in must be forgiven, as I am but a lover of the Regency era, not an expert.
The world was becoming smaller by the Regency period, and adventures to and from wild locations such as India were not exactly becoming commonplace, but were certainly much more attainable. I like to think of Hestia traversing the globe.
These are fictional characters, but they are characters who I really do love, so please be gentle with them.

OTHER BOOKS BY EMILY MURDOCH

Conquered Hearts Series
Conquests: Hearts Rule Kingdoms
Love Letters
Captives: Kingdoms Rule Hearts

or read them all in one volume:
Conquered Hearts: The Collection

Regency Romances
A Christmas Surprise
A Valentine Secret
A June Wedding
A Harvest Passion
Die Weihnachtsuberraschung (A Christmas Surprise translated into German)
Das Valentinsgeheimnis (A Valentine Secret translated into German)

Look out for more coming soon!

ABOUT THE AUTHOR

Emily Murdoch is a medieval historian and writer. Throughout her career so far she has examined a codex and transcribed medieval sermons at the Bodleian Library in Oxford, designed part of an exhibition for the Yorkshire Museum, worked as a researcher for a BBC documentary presented by Ian Hislop, and worked at Polesden Lacey with the National Trust. She has a degree in History and English, and a Masters in Medieval Studies, both from the University of York. Emily has just completed this four part Regency novella series, and is already writing a new full length historical novel.

You can follow her on twitter and instagram @emilyekmurdoch, find her on facebook at www.facebook.com/theemilyekmurdoch, and read her blog at www.emilyekmurdoch.blogspot.co.uk

Printed in Great Britain
by Amazon